MIDLIFE MOUNTAIN MOONSHINE

RENEE BRUME

Hot Mess Express Publishing

Cover: Getcovers.com

Editing: LM Wilkinson

Proofreading by: Horus Copyedit and Proofreading

Map by Piroska Edes behance.net/piroskaedes

CONTENTS

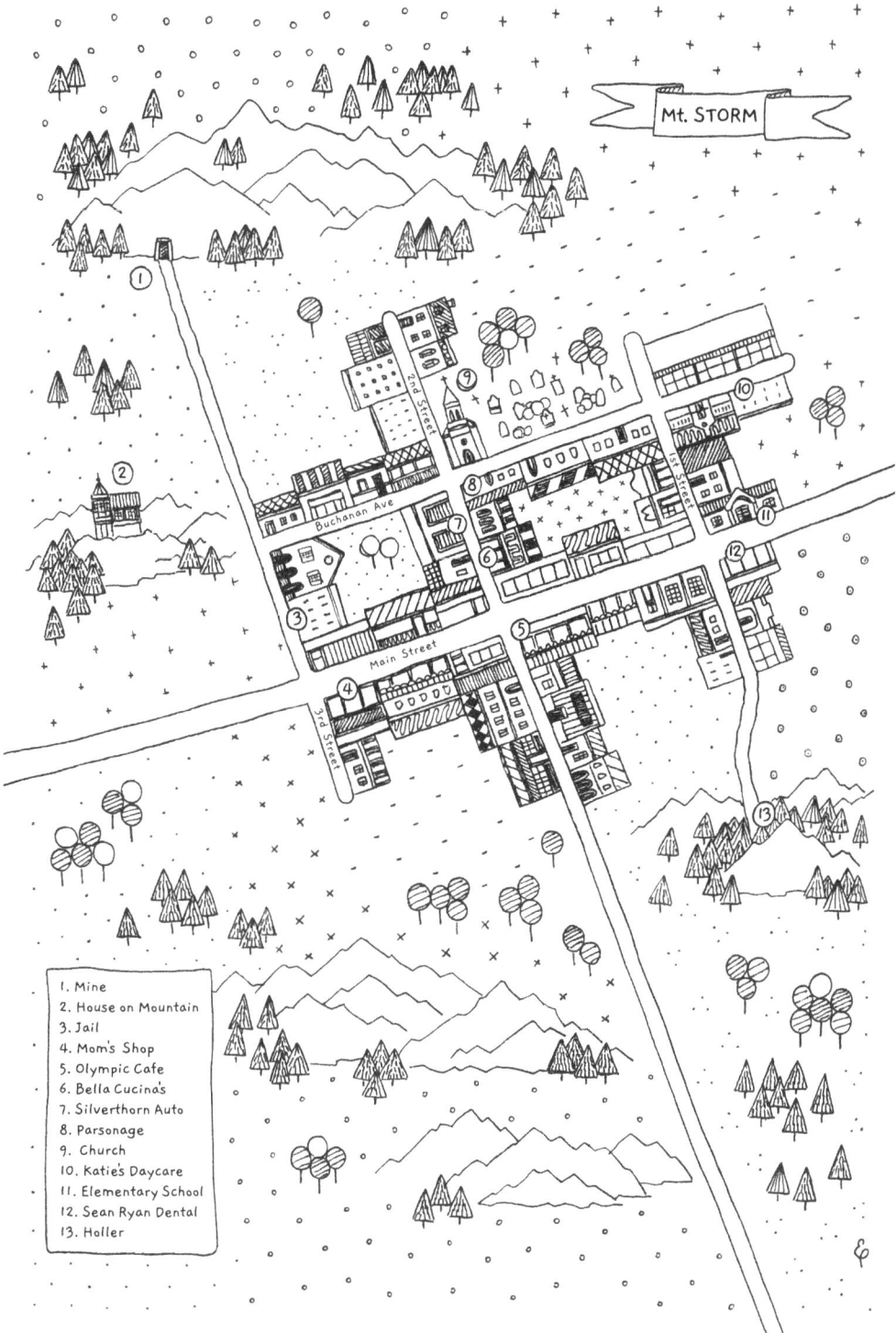

Mt. STORM

1. Mine
2. House on Mountain
3. Jail
4. Mom's Shop
5. Olympic Cafe
6. Bella Cucina's
7. Silverthorn Auto
8. Parsonage
9. Church
10. Katie's Daycare
11. Elementary School
12. Sean Ryan Dental
13. Holler

2nd Street
Buchanan Ave
1st Street
3rd Street
Main Street

CHAPTER 1
PACK

"My brother is a dumbass!" I howled, hitting my fist into the hard dash of my old Dodge pickup. Only, it wasn't a fist… it was a paw. The plastic under my hand shattered and I grimaced. In my anger, I had partially shifted into my wolf form.

I flexed my hand and shook it. I didn't mean to lose control of my temper like that. Taking a deep breath to calm myself, I shifted back to skin and bone, instead of fur and claw.

Shaking my head, I leaned back in my seat, looking out into the West Virginian hills that made up our pack land. My hip hurt from the hard bench seat of my truck, but it was just a touch of arthritis. I had just reached that magical age of 50 where, apparently, you start to fall apart, bit by bit.

My name is Sam Silverthorn, and I'm the leader of this rabble.

My family has lived here in these woods and on this land for generations, and we have a big secret.

We are all werewolves. The real genuine thing. Claws, fangs, and a short fuse, especially around the full moon. Which, checking the calendar, was tonight.

It was dusk, and the flickering of fireflies danced under the trees. Soon, the moon would rise and the pack would gather.

I leaned forward and rested my head on the steering wheel, the smell of the moonshine mash hanging in the air, wafting through the open window along with the night sounds. They had brewed this batch way too late. We needed it done last week.

If Junior didn't sell this batch soon, I might have to take a loan out from the friendly town leprechaun. No one wanted to owe money to Buster.

With a sigh, I rolled up the window, cutting off the smell and sounds. Putting my truck in gear, I cranked the wheel hard, listening to the power steering whine. I desperately needed a new truck, but I also desperately needed a few hundred thousand dollars. Neither was happening anytime soon.

There was a howl in the distance, and I smiled as I recognized the sound of my sister, Katie. Rolling down the window, I howled back. The pack was gathering.

My claws dug into the earth as I scrambled up the slope, the full moon shining down on my silver coat. I felt that twinge again in my hip and pushed back the pain.

Once at the top, I paused to catch my breath. My age was sneaking up on me—I wasn't a young pup anymore, that was for sure. I let my heart rate settle as I scanned the tree line below for my pack.

They must have gotten distracted. I lifted my silver muzzle

to the sky and let out a long mournful howl. It echoed through the valley below, hanging unanswered in the steamy West Virginia night.

I cocked my ears and listened, rewarded with answering howls from the forest. My mouth pulled up at the edges in a semblance of a smile, revealing my fangs. I lifted my head again, my nose pointed to the sky, and howled in answer.

Soon, my pack emerged from the deep woods below and scrambled up the loose slope to join me on the ridgeline.

I picked out my immediate brothers and sister, all with silver coats shining in the moonlight. It was our birthright and curse. We were born wolves but lived as humans.

I moved down the ridge, making space for them all. If a photographer were here, he would capture the grander picture —all of us standing like silver pillars against the light of the moon.

Together, in unison, we howled to the moon. Tonight, we were like a choir, lifting our voices into the night. She was a luminous beauty, hanging heavy in the sky. A Hunter's Moon— special because it marked the end of a wolf year. Tonight, we would feast, drink moonshine, and share stories. It was a special night for the pack.

And I, as leader, would sit at the head of the fire.

We raced through the woods, the hundreds of acres we held. Our moonshine stills hidden carefully in the rocky slopes, away from prying eyes. Countless times, the feds had come looking. They never found them. We were careful to hide them away, using magic older than time.

My brothers had taken over the business when my father died. I didn't like it, to be honest, but it was cold hard cash that kept the pack going.

The Silverthorns and the pack had never been rich, but we did all right. The eldest boys ran the shine, and the younger ones ran the auto body shop in town. My twin sister had made good—the only one of us to graduate from college. She ran Katie's Playhouse and Preschool in town.

And me? Well, I guess you could say my pops never expected much from me. I knew I was gay from a very young age. Everyone around me knew. It was obvious I didn't care much for the male wolves. But my pop was determined that "no daughter of his was going to do that gay stuff." He tried to set up an arranged marriage for me when I was 18 to the King Clan, to the north.

That's when I left home. I lived homeless in the woods of Kentucky. Meanwhile, my twin sister, Katie, married the man I was supposed to marry. I was banished, exiled, and no one saw me for years. I scraped together enough money to get my trucking license and disappeared into the long-haul trucking life.

But something in West Virginia always brought me back. My sister was my only connection to the family. I was living over in Winchester when I met my partner, Maggie, at a gay bar there.

Ironically, Maggie was living in Mount Storm. I needed to be with her, so I found my way back. Around that same time, my father died.

Looking over my pack, I knew this was where I wanted to be. Now that the old man was dead, my family begrudgingly welcomed me, some with wider arms. I somehow convinced the friendly side of the family to let me lead. My older brother, Junior, thought he was a shoo-in, and he was bitter that I tricked my mom into voting for me since that fateful day five years ago.

My dad was dead and gone, scattered to the wind in our

communal fire. I would like to think he would be proud of the leader I became, but who knows. He had some odd old-fashioned beliefs.

Now, I lead the pack down the ridge and to the game path that twisted through our woods. The crick bubbled along slowly to my left, low from lack of rain. We crossed, splashing easily through the shallow crossing, yipping and nipping at each other playfully.

Finally, with our Hunter's Moon patrol done, we rounded the corner of the trail and the small collection of houses that made up our community came into view.

Everyone was here, so the houses were dark, but I stepped into the clearing with the bonfire ring in the middle and changed back into my human form quickly. I brushed a hand through my short silver hair and turned my eyes to the pack as they changed one by one.

Soon, we surrounded the cold circle of stones. "Junior," I said to my eldest brother. "Could you get the fire?"

He grunted, throwing a few logs into the firepit, and then threw some matches down, their red ends arching into the night.

Randy, my other moonshining brother, pulled out his last quart jar of his best, and with a grin, held it up to the flickering firelight.

The smell of ash and campfire was in the air. I took the quart jar from him and pondered for a moment. "The gathering of the clan has begun." And then I took a sip.

I practically was weaned on moonshine, so the fire snaking down my throat didn't make me cough. I was pretty immune to it, to be honest, having built up a tolerance over the years. It would take more than just a few sips of Silverthorn's best to get me drunk.

I passed it on and watched each person take a sip before it ended up back with me. I threw a few sprinkles on the flames, watching it flare up. "For my old man, we pour out a few sips," I said, smiling at my mother, now an elder.

The family drew nearer to the fire and to me. I looked them over carefully. Junior was scowling, as usual. His sidekick in the shine business was Randy, who sat next to his wife, one hand protectively on her leg.

My two brothers who ran the auto shop, Frankie and Dennis, were my strongest allies, and they sat closest to me.

Katie sat next to her husband, Jonas King. Near them were their nearly adult children, who leaned forward eagerly to listen.

The smoke shifted, causing my eyes to burn. I waved it away with a dirty hand as the pack settled down. All eyes turned to me.

"Good evening. We gather tonight to discuss pack matters," I said and then I got right to business. "Junior, when will the next batch be done? We've got taxes to pay."

Junior shifted uncomfortably on the log. "Should be done by next Friday, but things might be too hot right now to sell the shine. Clyde over in Redhouse just got raided."

"Can we sell it outside of West Virginia?" I asked, looking at Katie and Jonas. Her husband instantly knew what I was talking about.

"I can make some arrangements," Jonas said carefully, glancing over at Junior and nodding.

"Crossing state lines is risky," Randy drawled slowly as if I didn't know the danger of going out of our home territory.

"We're fine. Our friendship with Potentia Security has protected us this long," I said, but internally, I knew we could be in trouble. The last few years, the feds had been all over the West

Virginia countryside, finding illegal stills right and left. They really hated it when they missed out on their taxes.

"It's foolish to expect Beth and friends to protect us forever," Katie said, a cross look on her face. Potentia Security—a government agency—used wizards, vampires, dragons, and a priest with holy water to safeguard the United States and the world from underworld demons. The Silverthorn pack had been their partners for years.

Well, that stung. My twin sister was dead smart. "It's still a goal of mine to take Silverthorn Moonshine and make it legal. But as you know, we need a lot of resources to do that. A building, expensive machinery, insurance, and permits. It's a big investment."

"I know," she said, her voice filled with frustration. "But it's the only way forward without one of the boys going to jail."

I sighed and then turned to my brothers who ran the auto business. "Dennis, Frankie. How's the shop?"

They looked at each other, concern on their faces, and then at me. "Not great. Business has been slow, and one of our lifts broke. The repair bill wiped out what savings we had."

"Shit," I mumbled to myself, not wanting to meet my clan's eyes. Oh, why did I step forward to take this job? I should have just let Junior have it. The problem was that Junior was as dumb as a box of rocks. I doubted we would have made it this far with him as the head of the pack.

"Well, sis… what's the monthly distribution?" Randy asked, leaning forward.

Every month, we divided up the profits among the families of the pack, which was what we lived on. "I have to pay the taxes," I said with a sigh. "The payout is $120 per family this month."

The pack grumbled, low at first, and then rising to near shouts. "We can't survive on that!"

"Listen, I don't know what to tell you all. We can use the food pantry. We'll do pack potlucks, and we can hunt," I said, sadness filling me. I didn't want my pack to struggle, but there was no other option. "And next month, when we sell the shine, the dispersal will be larger. Let's hope Junior and Randy get a good price."

There was muttering and angry sighs around the campfire, but times had been tough before. We knew how to do this. Randy leaned over to Junior and whispered something in his ear, then smirked at me.

"I think you should step down," Junior said suddenly, and instantly, everyone went quiet.

I felt my blood boil and I swallowed my anger, turning my attention to Junior, who was slouched down, sitting on a stump with his feet spread in front of him.

"And who should replace me, Junior? You, I suppose?" I said, taunting him. "You're a thorn in my side… you're just jealous that the voting went my way."

"Maybe we should have another vote?" he drawled, leaning forward, his hands resting on his knees.

"Who here thinks Junior can do a better job than I can?" I said, sarcasm dripping from my voice. There was no show of hands. "Well, I think that answered your question. Pack night is over."

I stood up and walked past the stone fire ring, seeing more moonshine come out. The mothers and children slipped away. My four brothers would stay up late tonight, drinking, playing cards, and talking shit about me. That's okay, I had thick skin.

"Sam," Katie said quietly, following me out of the stone ring. "Can we talk? I'm worried about you."

"I've got to get back to Maggie," I said, not breaking stride as I headed for my truck.

"How's she doing?" Katie asked to my retreating back.

"Not good, Katie. Not good at all."

"Let me know if there is anything I can do," she said to me. I didn't answer her. I couldn't. There was nothing she could do. Maggie was dying.

CHAPTER 2
MAGGIE

I parked my truck around the back of Maggie's Clip and Cut, next to the dumpster we shared with Dunn's Donuts. Mike Dunn was throwing out his trash, the big black bag making a meaty thunk into the nearly empty container.

"Sam, how are things?" Mike asked, brushing his hand off on a flour-covered apron.

I let out a deep sigh. "Not great, Mike. I've got hot flashes, bad knees, and too many bills. If you are asking about Maggie, she's hanging in there," I admitted, fishing out my keys and looking anxiously toward the back entrance. I could see the nurse already there, waiting for me.

"Stop by tomorrow, pick up a dozen on me," he said kindly, a sad smile on his face.

"Thanks. Maybe she'll be tempted to eat," I said, jiggling my keys in my hand and shifting my weight on my feet. The hospice nurse picked up her bag and opened the door.

"I'll let you go. Send my well wishes to Maggie, will you?" Mike said, turning back to the door of his donut shop.

"Of course," I said, glad to be done with the pleasantries. He meant well, but it was exhausting constantly giving people updates.

The nurse met me halfway up the walk. She was sent by the hospice company and stayed with Maggie every afternoon. Clara Hatch was long past retirement, with grey hair in a tight bun, she carried her purse in one hand and a medical bag in the other. I knew for a fact that her purse held a jar of Silverthorn Moonshine. She bought from us and always smelled vaguely of hooch.

"The doctor called in pain meds, but they won't be ready to pick up until tomorrow morning. She had a few bites of soup for dinner, and she's sleeping right now."

"Thank you," I said with a curt nod. I knew she would have left detailed notes inside, and the less I had to talk about it, the better. Clara would be anxious to head home to watch her shows and drink her moonshine.

"Goodnight," Clara said, moving off to her car, a little late-model Honda.

I hurried inside. My brother, Dennis, had taken an afternoon off a few weeks ago to help me clean out the office area. There, we had set up a hospital bed. A little bathroom down the hall was quickly retrofitted with handrails. It would have to do—Maggie couldn't navigate the stairs up and down every day.

Besides, the salon had been shuttered for months now. Maggie had taken out a second mortgage to pay the bills. She was counting on the large life insurance policy her old boss took out for her years ago to pay everything off once she died.

I peeked into the room. The nurse was wrong—Maggie was not asleep. She opened her eyes, "Hey," she said, her voice sounding rough.

"Hey," I said, trying to muster cheerfulness into my voice. "You need a drink?"

"Please." She reached out a long skeletal hand. The cancer had spread, it was all through her body now.

I held her water pitcher up and shook it. Empty. "I'm running upstairs to refill this. Want anything else while I'm up there?"

"No," she said with a sigh, closing her eyes.

Upstairs. It seemed like a whole different world now. The life we had built together graced the walls. The two of us, our arms around each other, smiling. During our trip to Seattle, we stayed with Russ Wright and his sasquatch family. They were wonderful hosts and gave us a tour of the Mount Rainer area, where they lived. We joked it had been the honeymoon we never had.

A tear came to my eye. *Why didn't we ever marry? Pure laziness, I guess.* I filled the pitcher in our small kitchen, grabbing a few ice cubes from the tray and chucking them in. Gazing at the kitchen table, I saw a mountain of mail. Bills, bills, and more bills.

Through the front room was our bedroom. The big queen bed called my name—I was exhausted. But for weeks now, I had been sleeping on a cot downstairs, next to Maggie's bed, just in case she needed anything.

The pitcher filled, I headed back downstairs and topped up her Twilight coffee mug. Team Jacob, of course.

She picked up the coffee mug, her hand shaking, and held it to her mouth. She drank deeply and passed it back to me, spilling a few drops down her front.

I sat it down carefully on the nightstand, pushing aside dozens of orange pill bottles. Then I took her hand, stroking it gently. "Maggie, we don't have much time left."

"I know," she said, closing her eyes. Her small hand in mine gave me a squeeze, what little energy she could muster.

"Marry me," I said softly, holding her fragile little hand in mine.

Her eyes snapped open, and a small smile came to her thin mouth. "Marry? You want to make me an honest woman?"

"In the worst way," I said, a chuckle on my lips.

"I don't know..." Maggie said, staring at me with her brown eyes. Her hair, once dyed pink, was coming in patchy since the doctors had given up on chemo.

"October 9th is in a few days. Seems fitting we should get married on the anniversary of when gay marriage became legal in the state of West Virginia." I hated the way my voice sounded pleading. "I never thought I would get married. I never thought it was necessary. But I want the world to know we loved each other."

She blinked her eyes. So rarely did we talk of her impending demise. "If it would make you happy," she said, touching the ring I had given her years ago on that trip to Seattle. "I guess we are married in our hearts, anyway. I don't see why we need a piece of paper."

"I need the piece of paper. Plus, it will make the estate just that much easier," I said, thinking of the pile of papers upstairs —her will and testament, power of attorney, etc. We had all the paperwork in order, but you never knew.

"Okay then," she said, reaching out and taking my hand again. "If you'll take me, sick and halfway in the grave."

"I wouldn't have it any other way," I said, my throat closing up painfully. *No, I didn't want to burst into tears now.* With every cell in my body, I willed myself to hold it together.

Her eyes closed again, but now she had a smile on her face. "I'm tired," she said.

"It's bedtime now," I whispered and leaned over to kiss my beautiful partner on the forehead.

It was a long night, and I was glad to see the hospice nurse arrive the next day, new pain pills in hand.

I went back upstairs and sat on the bed, running my hands over the rainbow cover. I should be getting ready for my day as it was going to be a busy one. I needed to talk to the Lutherans... they married gay couples, last I heard.

I took the quickest of showers, lathering my silver hair with the citrus-scented expensive stuff from the retail stocks downstairs. Listen... if we were going to lose everything, my hair might as well look good.

I was just sitting down at the table, the nasty bills spread out in front of me—a mountain of red—when the buzzer for the outside door rang.

Thinking it was odd that we had guests, I ran to the intercom system and pressed the button, "Yes?" I asked, wishing the video screen hadn't broken. I had no money to fix it.

"It's Beth. I'm here with Eliana. Sorry for the short notice, but I had an appointment cancel last minute."

"Of course," I said, hastily mashing the open button. I glanced around quickly and then went and closed the bathroom door with the mirror hanging on the wall.

Beth Potentia came tromping up the stairs from below. She was about the same age as Maggie, 52. She was already going salt and pepper, but she looked good in a pair of black jeans and a teal blouse.

Her adopted daughter, Eliana, looked like the little angel she was. At six, she was just starting school. Beth had worked something out with the school system and she was able to attend normal school, just like everyone else. I remember her telling me she had to meet with the superintendent of the schools and have all the mirrors taken out. They told all the parents it was because kids kept wrecking the bathrooms as part of an online challenge, but we knew it was to protect Eliana.

Eliana smiled up at me, her black curls around her face and her dark eyes twinkling. "I drew a picture for Maggie," she said, quietly holding out a folded piece of paper.

"Thank you. I'm sure she will love that," I said, smiling at the sweet child. I had spent more time looking after this girl than she knew, running patrols around this town, making sure her real father didn't find her.

The kicker was that her real father was Satan himself. He wanted his daughter back, and so far, had been pretty adamant about being a pain in the butt for everyone in Potentia Security. He had the uncanny ability to appear in mirrors and fire, and if either was big enough, he could use it as a portal to step through.

"How are things?" I asked Beth, standing in the living room. We hadn't talked in a week or so, which was odd.

"Oh, you know… busy as always. Easton has been out, he tweaked his knee down in the mines the other day, so we've all been pulling extra terminal duty. I have a trip to DC coming up next week. I've been meaning to contact you. Would you be willing to set the pack up for 24-hour surveillance while I'm gone?"

"Of course," I said. "How long is your trip?"

"I'm leaving on Tuesday, but it's just the one day in DC. Then I have to fly to Seattle and meet with Russ and his family. They're working with the Canadian government on an issue they've been having in British Columbia. I'll be gone about a week," Beth said, looking over at Eliana. Then she frowned, "I'm sorry, I shouldn't be asking for help. You have a lot on your plate."

"No, the pack could use the funds. If I'm being honest, we are in a pinch," I admitted, running my hands through my hair. I gestured toward the pile of bills. "The one on the top is the bank asking for money. If I don't figure something out, they are going to foreclose on this place."

"Oh, Sam. Please let me help," Beth said, her eyes filling with tears.

"You've already done more than enough, but those are just bandages. There is no getting around that Maggie's Clip and Cut is not going to open again. I'll have to sell the building as we are way too behind on the mortgage payment."

"I'd hate to see that happen," Beth said, dabbing at her eyes.

"Yeah, me too, but there are a lot of things that have been tough lately." I hesitated and then glanced at her. "Maggie and I are getting married. It's going to be a small wedding, but I know she would want you there."

"I wouldn't miss it for the world," Beth said with a shaky smile.

"Oh, Mom. Can I come? Can I be the flower girl? I've always wanted to be a flower girl!" Eliana said, jumping up and down so that her curls bounced.

"It's not that fancy, but of course you can be the flower girl," I said, laughing. "Now, you're in luck because Maggie is up and feeling better this morning. The doctor prescribed her some new meds. Why don't you head downstairs with this drawing and pay her a visit."

CHAPTER 3
CONTROL

I swallowed my pride and stared at the tall white church on the corner of Buchanan Ave and Second Street. Behind it, I could see the quiet graveyard, shaded by the huge maple trees that dotted the area. A lump rose in my throat and I shook my head, not wanting to think of the inevitable.

The parsonage was just across the street, a sweet little bungalow framed by climbing ivy. The pastor's wife, Amanda, was in the front garden. She was wearing a big floppy hat and was nearly elbow-deep in the dirt.

In the backyard, I could hear her three little snot goblins shrieking loudly. All boys, and all with more energy than they knew what to do with. A teen boy, with the same blond hair as his mother, ran into the front yard, furiously shooting a water gun at his younger brothers.

"Boys, please," Amanda said, wiping the sweat off her forehead with the back of her arm. "Keep it down." She caught me watching them and then smiled as she stood. "You must be Sam. David said you were coming. He's over at the church. He should be in the office."

"Thank you," I said as the teen ran into the backyard, screaming about getting revenge.

I entered the church, feeling the coolness of the interior. In my life, I had only been in these halls a few times. The last time I was here was for Beth and Dan's wedding. That had been a good party.

My skin prickled. I was never quite comfortable in churches, being cursed with lycanthropy and all, but contrary to popular belief, we could walk over the threshold. We were pretty indestructible—fire and silver bullets being our only weaknesses. And since silver bullets weren't common, I was pretty safe.

I couldn't remember exactly where the office was. Pushing through some side double doors, I made my way down a short hall, passing a bathroom and a nursery for the little ones. My instincts were right because at the end was the church office.

A mean-looking old woman sat at the front desk, dressed in the most hideous orange magnolia flower dress I had ever seen. Her look was completed with a lace pilgrim collar and shoes so respectable, they almost sat up and saluted you. Her blue hair was piled high on her head, giving her the appearance of more height than she probably had. She was chewing on the end of a pen, idly looking out the window before she spotted me.

She snapped to attention, "Hello. You shouldn't sneak up on people," she said, her voice rude.

"My apologies. I have an appointment with the pastor," I said, feeling ill at ease under her stern glare. A sign on her desk read Isadora Snucks.

She looked me up and down, eyeing my jeans and flannel shirt, and sniffed. "Who should I tell him is calling?"

"Sam Silverthorn," I said firmly, meeting her eyes. Darned if I was going to be bullied by a mean old lady.

Isadora frowned and then picked up her phone, holding it to her ear and dialing a series of digits angrily, smashing them down. "Pastor Etherridge, you have a guest to see you."

She put down the phone and then picked up a sudoku book and her pen, furiously scribbling the answers. I stood there, glancing back at the door.

"Well, what are you waiting for? He'll see you now," she said with an irritated sigh, pointing to the door with the back of her pen, which had nearly been chewed into oblivion.

Feeling slightly off and peeved, I made my way back to the door, opening it carefully. The pastor sat at his desk, wearing a tie and white shirt, but with the sleeves rolled up. A blazer hung on the coat hook next to the door.

The office was nicely furnished. Bookcases, filled with religious reference books, lined the walls. A brass lamp graced his desk and the hunter green carpet screamed early 00s, as did the wallpaper. Fancy, but dated.

"Miss Silverthorn. Lovely of you to join me today. Please have a seat," he said jovially, standing briefly to welcome me with a hearty handshake. He had soft hands and the grin of a man who was trying to sell you something.

"I hope Isadora didn't scare you. She isn't great with people, but she's worked for the church for decades, and frankly, the board wouldn't hear of me replacing her. I tried to encourage her to retire, but she claims we couldn't live without her."

"Oh," I said, biting my lip, unsure how to ask this priest to marry Maggie and I.

"Well, you said you wanted to speak to me about a personal matter?" he prompted, his eyebrow raising. "How is Maggie doing? Did you want to discuss the funeral arrangements?"

I blinked, taken aback. "Umm," I muttered, my tongue getting tied up.

"It's okay. This is a tough time for you, I'm sure. Maggie was baptized here, and her mother attended regularly. I should really go out and offer her some comfort." He reached over the desk, taking my hand and patting it gently.

I pulled back, my skin buzzing from his touch. If he noticed, he didn't comment. Instead, he sat back, waiting for me to speak.

"Well, sir. That's a great thought, but Maggie and I have already talked about what she wants. What I'm here for, actually, is to ask you to marry us. My understanding is that the Lutherans will marry gay couples."

"Oh, well." Now it was his turn to stumble. He flushed and shifted in his seat. "I didn't think this issue would come up, to be honest."

"Is there a problem?" I asked, feeling panicked as I clutched the arms of the chair.

"To understand, I have to give you a bit of a history lesson. Our denomination recognizes that all people are created by God and are welcome to take part fully in church life."

"Great," I said, a smile coming to my face. "As Maggie has been a member of this congregation for as long as she's been alive, you shouldn't have a problem marrying us."

"Well, there is a problem… I'm opposed to it, as is our board."

The smile slipped off my face. I knew what was coming. "Your decision then?"

"Well, I suppose I would be forced to do the ceremony, but I insist it must be offsite and away from everyone's eyes. But my other issue is not with your queerness, it's with your werewolfism. You are cursed. I can't bless the union of a human and a foul werewolf. It wouldn't be right."

I took a shuttering breath and stood. Anger thrummed

through me and I looked down in horror at my hands, which were now both claws.

Pastor Etherridge yelped and scrambled back—his face shocked.

Air filled my lungs and I stilled myself, willing my claws to turn back into hands. Shifting out of anger was becoming an annoying habit of mine recently. Normally, I had firm control. "My apologies. I've been through a lot of stress lately." I held up both hands to show him I meant him no harm.

But that didn't seem to calm him. He was practically hugging the wall. "Get out," he said in a shaky voice, pointing to the door. "You are not welcome in this house."

"Fine," I said, tears coming to my eyes. "Is Maggie's funeral plot refundable? I don't want her buried in such a bigoted place."

"Yes," he said, squeezing his eyes shut. "I'll have Isadora mail you a check."

"Fine," I said with a sinking heart. I left immediately, not uttering a word to Isadora on my way out. She was so engrossed in her sudoku that she didn't even notice me sailing by.

Halfway to my truck parked on the street, I lost control of my shifting, fully turning into a werewolf. A car shuddered to a stop as I blindly crossed the street, missing me by inches.

The driver yelled and laid on his horn. I wanted to bite, tear, hunt, and howl. Anger coursed through my veins. I passed my truck, not desiring to shift back into my human form. My body stretched out as I ran, my claws making a scratching noise against the asphalt.

Passing people on the sidewalk, I heard their gasps. It was

not often a werewolf was seen in the town in broad daylight. In the back of my mind, some semblance of reason remained, and I knew I needed to get out of sight. Luckily, my brother's auto shop was just down the street, so I picked up my pace, the wind against my face.

The doors of the garage were open and I ran in, nearly bowling over both of my brothers. Dennis and Frankie were hunched over an old Mustang, elbow-deep in engine grease when I came tearing in. I loved the smell of the garage—oil, grease, and gas. It brought back memories of the time I had spent driving trailers around the country.

"Whoa!" Dennis said, nearly hitting his head on the hood of the car. "Sam, what in the hell are you doing?"

Frankie glanced around, catching one of his employee's eyes. "Jerry, close the garage!" he bellowed and then turned to me, "You, in the office!" he commanded, pointing to their small office.

Bounding toward it, I lifted my muzzle in a howl filled with all the sorrow and pain I could muster. Dang, that felt good. I did it again and again before dropping on all fours to the cold cement, feeling the anger drain out of my body.

I felt myself shift back into my human form. Now, I was curled up on the cold cement floor, my eyes firmly closed. My brothers came in, shut the door, and closed the blinds to the window that looked out on the auto bay.

Frankie leaned beside me, bringing me into a hug. I didn't even mind that he was greasy and smelled like motor oil. "Frankie," I sobbed. "She's dying... and—" My voice broke.

Dennis stood with his arms crossed, looking angry. "Who hurt my sister? Who do I need to teach a lesson?"

A choked chuckle escaped my throat. "I'm sorry. That was

terrible and unprofessional. I shouldn't have just shifted like that. I was just so upset."

Frankie shrugged. "It happens to the best of us. Now, what happened?"

He stood and helped me up, leading me to a mangy brown and tan plaid couch with missing legs. He shooed the shop cat, Jinx, away.

Jinx brushed up against my ankles like he was saying he was sorry, before settling in an empty cardboard brake rotor box that had been left by the trashcan.

I told Frankie and Dennis the entire story of my terrible visit with Pastor Etherridge. They listened to every word in silence. Halfway through, Dennis reached into his office drawer and pulled out a mason jar of moonshine, unscrewing the top and passing it to me. I took a sip, feeling the fire loosen my tongue as it went down.

As I finished my story, my tears were gone, along with the moonshine. Empty and sad, I placed the jar on the edge of the desk and let out an enormous sigh. "It's just so disappointing. I know we can get married at the courthouse, but it's not the same."

Frankie and Dennis exchanged a look. "Listen, we didn't realize how bad Maggie had gotten. We knew she was sick, but it's not like you share your personal life with us. You don't even bring Maggie to pack night."

I laughed, hanging my head. "What's she going to do? Sit around the fire and listen to us howl in the distance?"

Frankie paused for a moment before speaking, "There is a way to cure her, you know."

"What do you mean?" I asked, suddenly feeling 100% sober.

Dennis tripped over himself, trying to explain, "Well, you

know, we didn't want to bring it up as it's dangerous. And we were hoping the doctors could cure her."

"What do you mean?" I demanded, my voice rising. "Tell me, Dennis."

"You can change her into a werewolf," Dennis said, and the answer fell like a bomb between us.

CHAPTER 4
FAMILY

The sun hit the mason jar of moonshine, splitting the light into a rainbow that spilled across my arm. I made my way to Silverthorn land right after talking to my brothers and settling down.

I found the pack hard at work bottling up the newest batch of moonshine, sealing them tight, and placing them in wooden crates for transportation.

Randy and Junior were leading this operation, set back in one of the ramshackle houses that leaked like a sieve and was past the point of being worth fixing.

Junior growled when he saw me, his lips curling up in disgust. "You decide to finally come and help us? We could use it. Four batches were done today. That's a good 30-50 gallons that need to be jarred up."

"Well, I really came to talk to Mom, but of course, I'll help," I said, taking the offered apron and wrapping it around my waist.

An hour later, I was hot and sweaty and my back sore. The jars were packed up and Junior placed the last crate in the back room, all ready for transport.

"Don't lose this batch. We need it," I warned, doing mental math and figuring out which bills were a priority.

"You worry too much, sister," Randy said. "Are you staying for dinner? They caught a deer earlier, and Mom is baking some apple pies."

"That sounds good. I really need to get home to Maggie, but…" I bit my lip. If I was going to change her, I should at least give the pack a heads-up. "Yeah, I'll stay. Where's Mom?"

"She's in the big house," Junior said, nodding down the dirt lane toward our childhood home.

"I need to talk to her," I said, turning toward the familiar structure. The house was crafted by my father's hands—the wooden siding, the roof, everything done with werewolf power. Inside was small but cozy, with an enormous stone fireplace in the common area, a spacious kitchen, just one bathroom, and a loft upstairs for us kids. Hard to believe that all eight of us once fit in this little home.

Opening the screen door, I called inside, "Mom!"

"Back here," I heard her voice and instantly knew she was in the kitchen. Making my way through the common room, I saw not much had changed. The long table still stood, empty now, rarely filled except at Christmas and Thanksgiving. The head of the table always left empty in honor of my father, who died six years ago in a fire while working for Potentia Security.

The kitchen was warm and the windows were all open, a slight breeze doing little to take the heat from the oven out of the air. Air conditioning was a dirty word around here. No one wanted to pay the electricity costs. Six pies were cooling on the chipped counter top.

"I don't know how you do it with no AC," I said, fanning my already flustered face.

"I'm used to it," Mom said, wiping her wrinkled hands on a

kitchen towel. "I just put the last two pies in the oven. Are you staying for dinner?" Her black hair, now with gray strands, was pulled back into a loose braid, which hung far down her back.

"Maybe," I said, thinking about getting back to Maggie.

"It's teatime," Mom said, pulling tea bags out of the drawer. Lemon ginger—her favorite. "I'll pour you a mug. Sit with me."

Not giving me time to protest, she plopped the tea bags into two clay mugs and poured hot water over the top. The fresh citrus smell filled the room and I gladly accepted the hot mug from her, even though I wished it was iced tea.

"Thank you, Mom," I said, taking a sip. It instantly took me back to my childhood, of being sick and in bed with peanut butter cookies and a mug of this tea.

"How's Maggie holding up?" Mom asked kindly, her eyes full of concern as she sat across from me at the small table in the middle of the kitchen.

I sighed, wrapping my hands around the body of the mug. "Not good. I went into town today to talk to Pastor Etherridge about marrying us. He wouldn't do it."

"Because you're a gay couple?" she asked softly, her eyes full of hurt.

"No… because I'm a werewolf."

"Oh." She snorted. "Ridiculous. Well, you know how those religious types feel about us."

"Yeah. Like we have something contagious," I said, picking up the mug and taking a slow drink. "Mom. Dennis brought up something I hadn't considered…"

She paused with her drink halfway to her mouth, her eyes staring at me.

"He said if I changed Maggie into a werewolf, it would cure her of the cancer."

She put her mug down gently and folded her hands together, not meeting my eyes. "That is true. But there are massive risks."

Instantly, I became angry. A low growl tore out of my throat. "Why didn't anyone tell me? You have all just watched her suffer… watched *me* suffer, while she's fought this cancer? Now you tell me I could have cured her with a little bite?"

Mom shifted in her seat and then reached over and squeezed my hand. "It hasn't been done in a very long time, and like I said, it's incredibly dangerous. In history, a person was changed into a werewolf only after an attack didn't kill them. That's how the packs grew. Over time, we became more civilized and wanted to live in society, not at the edges, so we stopped killing humans for sport and pleasure. Plus, I like to think the women put a stop to it."

"You could argue we still live at the edges," I mumbled, pulling my hand back. "Tell me how to do it."

"Sam," she said in her *mom* voice. That voice you didn't argue with. The voice that told you to do your chores or finish your homework. "You might just end up killing her anyway."

"TELL ME!" I demanded, slamming my fist on the table. The mugs jumped.

Mom sucked in a deep breath. "You'll have to get permission from the pack."

"The last time I checked, I'm the leader. I'll do what I want," I said, gritting my teeth.

"Fine. Come with me," Mom said, getting up from the table. I stood, following her out of the kitchen. Instantly, I knew she was leading me to her bedroom. She opened the roughhewn door and we went inside.

The handmade bed, with one of her beautiful quilts covering it, stood in the middle of the room. Here, all of her children had been born. A dresser with a mirror was pushed against the wall, and she opened the drawer, pulling out a book that I had seen only a few times before—the Silverthorn Journal.

It was bound in old brown leather, now cracking with age. There was no title on the spine or front to tell the reader what it was. She laid it on the dresser top carefully and opened the front cover.

At first, the words inside were written in an almost indecipherable script. There was no intro, no title page, no table of contents. The first entry gave a date: May 6th, 1859.

"One time when we were little, Katie challenged me to sneak into your room and read this," I said, remembering the only time I had actually touched the forbidden tome.

"I remember. Your father found you," she said softly.

"He spanked me with his belt that day," I said. "He was going to spank Katie too, but I took her licks for her. I couldn't sit for a week."

"You always were the tough one," Mom said with a chuckle. "And the one willing to take risks."

I touched the parchment pages. If I tried really hard, I could make out the words.

My name is Rhett Silverthorn, and this is my journal. I was raised on a farm near Shepherdstown.

"That's the oldest town in West Virginia," I said, holding my place in the book.

"It is. Us Silverthorns have West Virginia in our blood," she said. "Keep reading."

When I was twenty, I was attacked one night while coming home from hunting. What I thought was a huge wolf creature jumped at me, biting me on the arm and bringing me down. Somehow, I survived, but when I awoke, it was the next morning and I was feverish. I lay in a puddle of my own blood, and strangely, my attacker was not found.

Making my way home, I had no idea what was in store for me. I was feverish and ill, and a day later, I found out what had been done to me.

My body twisted, and I shifted into a monster. I heard the howls in the distance as I changed into a werewolf. Unable to control myself, I killed my family, who were only trying to help me. For my entire life, I must live with that guilt.

In my sorrow, I burned the house down, and their bodies with it. Then I ran and joined the pack. My new family. Over time, I rose to the top, and now I'm the leader with pups of my own. This is our story.

I wanted to keep reading, but it would take me all day to get through this entire thing. I flipped to the end and found an entry from my father, just a month before his death, describing some work he was doing with Potentia Security.

"Why have you kept this from me?" I asked, closing the front cover gently.

"You weren't ready. Besides, it's almost full," she pointed out.

"I'll make a new one. Volume two," I said, knowing I would commission a leather book, just like this one, and maybe a sleeve or box to store them in.

"That has the answers you are looking for. But you need to talk to the pack before you do this. Maggie would be a member forever, especially if you intend to marry her."

"Thank you," I said, looking over at her old-fashioned alarm clock on the nightstand—the one that needed winding every day. "I'll talk to them at dinner."

━━

I called Clara Hatch, the hospice nurse, and begged her to stay later, off the clock from her service. She reluctantly agreed after I promised her two jars of Silverthorn's finest.

I sat at the long table in the grass with my brothers and the rest of the pack. Nearby, a picnic table groaned with the roasted venison, pies, potato salads, corn on the cob, and watermelon.

Katie sat down next to me, carrying two plates. She slid one over to me. "Eat," she commanded. "I made the potato salad. It's Mom's recipe."

I picked up a fork and dug in. Memories of my youth, spent at picnics just like this one, avoiding the boys and trying desperately to fit in with the girls, filled my mind.

"Mom! I'm supposed to meet Stacie at the mall!" my niece, Lauren, said with her cell phone in her hand, tossing her long hair.

"Stacie is just going to have to wait. This is a family event!" Katie said sharply.

Lauren stomped off to hang out with a group of teen werewolves. Her brother, Nick, looking too cool in a leather jacket and sunglasses, was leaning against his old Trans Am my brothers had helped him fix up. He looked straight out of the Teen Wolf movie.

Katie sighed. "Kids don't get any easier when they get older."

I laughed, "I wouldn't know, but you have great kids."

The rest of the pack filled their plates and ate. Mom arrived with two more pies, smiling and looking unruffled.

"I'm glad you came. You should come to these more often," Katie said, glancing over her shoulder at the desserts.

"Go for it. I won't tell," I said with a grin. As she got up, her husband, Jonas, slid over, looking like he wanted to talk.

"Hey, Jonas," I said, giving him a little wave. He was a quiet guy, the diplomat of our pack. He was often off on "business trips" to the north or west. Jonas would come back, with his quiet ways, and pass on requests from other packs. Usually, it was hunting agreements. We wouldn't go east of a certain spot. Years ago, we were supposed to marry each other. He married my sister instead. I'm glad it worked out for them.

"Hi," he said, gazing down intently at his venison. Forking it into his mouth, he mumbled, "The King Clan has made arrangements with your brothers to buy the entire batch of moonshine. They are going to sell it at a premium in our area. It's a favor, really."

"I know. Thank you," I said sincerely. "It's really going to help the pack."

"You should look into making the moonshine into a legal operation," Jonas said. His reddish-brown hair was wavy and fell to his collar. He wore a baseball cap and sports glasses, balanced on the brim. There was intelligence behind those green eyes. Even though he wasn't a Silverthorn, I respected him.

"People keep telling me that," I said, running my hand through my short hair. "I would need a lot of money. We would need a building, expensive equipment, proper branding, and not to mention the state and federal licensing."

"They have these things called banks," Jonas said, his green eyes teasing me.

"Can't get a loan unless I put the Silverthorn land up as collateral. I'm not willing to risk it."

"I respect that, I guess," Jonas said, nodding.

Katie came back with two slices of pie balanced on her arms. "Hey, you stole my spot!"

"I'll give it back for a piece of that pie," Jonas teased, holding out his hand.

"Oh, fine!" She laughed and handed him a piece of pie. "This was for Sam. I'll let her get her own."

"Hey!" I protested. "I thought you were my twin sister!"

"I am, but this is PIE!" Katie said, throwing her head back so that her long silver hair swung free as she sat on the bench.

"Here, Sam. I've got you," Mom said, bustling over. "I wrapped up a whole pie for you and Maggie."

"What! She gets a WHOLE pie! No fair!" Randy said, looking over from the table next to us.

"I need to get back soon anyway. The nurse is staying late," I said, standing up and accepting the pie. My mouth went dry as I realized it was now or never.

I cleared my throat, holding on to the edge of the pie pan like it was a buoy. One by one, everyone went quiet and turned toward me.

"Jonas just gave me the good news—the King Clan bought the entire batch of Silverthorn's best," I said, looking around at my pack with a grin. There were the expected hoots and hollers as they realized the payout next month was going to be a good one. I waited a moment for everyone to quiet down again. "Now, I have something personal I want to bring to the pack. As many of you know, Maggie has been fighting cancer."

I heard people say, "Bless her," and, "We're praying for you."

I held up my hand. "I appreciate your love and concern, but she doesn't have long… which is why I'm coming to you today. I'm going to try something, and I need your support."

Katie looked at me with enormous eyes. She knew exactly what I was going to say. It was that twin thing, which had proved useful many times as children. Now, not so much.

"Sam," she whispered. "You can't do this."

"I can," I said. "I'm going to change Maggie into a werewolf. Or at least, I'm going to try. Not much to lose, to be honest."

Immediately, there was a reaction. Junior, who had been at the back table with his buddies, stood up, his overalls hanging off from one strap. His face reddened and his fists tightened at his sides. "How dare you! There hasn't been a human turned into a werewolf in a good century!"

I held up my hand. "I've made up my mind. Please accept her into the pack, it's all I ask."

Junior stomped up to the front. I stood, with my arms crossed, staring him down. Things had been tense between us for a while, ever since I "stole" the pack leadership from him years ago. The problem is, it was common knowledge that Junior wasn't very bright. His one skill was brewing up moonshine. He had the family recipes memorized. Not even Randy had that knowledge.

"We won't allow this to happen!" Junior said, spittle flying. Randy jumped up, rolled his eyes, and held Junior back with one hand.

"Who is "we" Junior?" I asked, cocking my head. His little clique was giving me cold looks, but none of them said a word.

"I demand a pack vote," Junior said, shaking Randy off.

"Fine." I gestured toward the pack. "You all know Maggie. You love her like a sister. Tell me you want to let her die." There was mumbling and I watched, pie in hand, as they conversed. Junior went to his table of friends and had an animated conversation, complete with gesturing and stomping of feet.

I waited for what seemed like an eternity and then put two fingers to my lips, letting out a piercing whistle. "Show of hands, who thinks I should try to change Maggie?"

My heart filled with happiness as the majority of the pack raised their hands solemnly. Mom and Katie stood next to me, their hands held high. My brothers, excluding Junior, joined them.

I looked over at Junior and his group of buddies, the only holdouts. "Are you going to be a problem?"

"No," he said, his eyes narrowing.

"Good, I would hate to exile my own brother," I said. Internally, I was fearful of a showdown with him. If he pushed it, I would be forced to act, and I didn't want to do that.

"You need to watch your tone with me," Junior said. He stood up, grabbed his baseball cap from the tabletop, and stomped off toward his house.

CHAPTER 5
WARNING

I drove back home that night with the wind in my hair, the old book by my side, belting out The Chick's version of Landslide.

I turned down Main Street as tears came to my eyes. Darn song, making me feel things. This was my home, and dang it, I would fight for it and my pack.

Pulling in around Clara Hatch's old car, I jumped out and grabbed the book. For once, I had a smile on my face.

The alleyway was dark, with just a few fixtures on the back of the building emitting pools of light. Honestly, my mind was so on telling Maggie my plan that I didn't see the shadow.

"Werewolf… ssstop," the voice hissed, and I nearly jumped out of my skin. Standing in the darkness was a tall, pale man with black hair and intense eyes.

"Who are you?" I asked weakly, taking a few steps back.

"I am Jesus Armando, leader of a vampire clan in the holler. Surely, you've heard of us?"

I licked my lips, my eyes going wide. Everything in me wanted to shift. My nerves screamed danger. Vampires and werewolves had been mortal enemies since the beginning of time. Instead, I took another step back. "I have heard of you. Beth Potentia told me about you and warned us to stay out of the holler as that's your territory. What do you want?"

"I'm not going to hurt you. But your familia aren't staying out of the holler... your brothers," he said in a thick Spanish accent.

My eyes narrowed. "What about my brothers? Which ones?" I said, my heart thumping.

"The one they call Junior, and the other one... his shadow. Keep your perros out!"

"How dare you call my brothers dogs!" I said, my hackles rising and my teeth baring.

"You should watch them. Your brothers are no bueno," Jesus said, raising his hands to show he didn't intend to attack me.

"What do you mean?" I asked, feeling my hair settle back into place. I smoothed it down with a hand, taking a few deep breaths.

"They are doing bad deals with the carteles. Me and my clan try to keep the drugs out, but it's a losing battle. The carteles have lots of gun power. Messing with them is muerte," he said, making a slashing motion across his neck.

"Cartels? Drugs? Oh, shit," I said, realization dawning on me.

"You deal with them? Save me the problemo?" Jesus asked as a car turned down the alley, the lights illuminating his pale face. He drew up an arm, shading his eyes from the glare.

"Si," I nodded.

Without a word, he stepped back into the darkness, and with a flutter of wings and a flash of purple, he transformed into a raven. I could make him out, soaring into the air and disappearing into the dark of the new moon.

"Shit," I said again, rubbing my forehead. Well, there was nothing I could do about it. I needed to relieve Nurse Hatch, who was probably two sheets to the wind right now.

I was next to Maggie, sitting up against the headboard. A late show was on, but the volume was turned so low I couldn't hear it. The television was filling the room with flickering light as the host smiled and laughed at his guest silently.

The bed was tight, but she was thin. Too damn thin.

The journal lay between us. She lifted her head—her brown hair had been washed and braided back. "Change me, Sam," she said, her eyes sparkling.

"Hold on now," I said, biting my lip. "I'm a little worried. What if something goes wrong? What if blood lust overtakes me and I..."

"Accidentally kill me?" Maggie finished my thought, tilting her head. "It doesn't matter. I'll be dead, anyway," she said those words in such a happy, lilting voice it broke my heart.

I picked up the book and opened it to the paragraph that described the process, from an entry dab smack in the middle of the civil war.

It starts with a simple bite that breaks the skin. From there, the wound will begin to bubble and fester, the person will run a high fever for a few days, then slip into unconsciousness. When they awake, they will transform into a werewolf. They must feed, or they will turn on anyone who approaches.

"What if something goes wrong, Maggie? I couldn't live with myself. What if someone else gets hurt, or God forbid, a little kid?" I said, dread rising in me. This entry was clear, back in the days of the Wild West, werewolf packs of newly changed humans wandered the deserts and prairies.

The historical near extermination of wolves across the US was a knee-jerk reaction to this. Not that wolves were at fault, but it did send our packs into hiding and caused us to stop hunting humans.

"It won't," she said with a smile. Leaning over to me, she kissed me on the lips. I wrapped my arms around her and closed my eyes.

"I'm afraid you won't survive the high fever. You're so weak as it is."

She touched my lips with one thin finger. "Do it now. Before you chicken out."

I looked at the calendar. "Potentia Security wants us to work next week. How about on Friday when Beth gets back? I'll clear my schedule, and then I can babysit baby pup Maggie. To be honest, Nurse Hatch would probably like the week off."

She smiled. "Fine. I wouldn't want to eat Clara, anyway. She's well pickled with Silverthorn Moonshine."

We both laughed and then finished reading the journal together. She drifted off to sleep on my arm, her brown hair falling over her face. I smoothed it back, tucked her in, and then went upstairs to our lonely bed. It took me a while to fall asleep, my mind whirling with a thousand what-ifs.

Somewhere in the distance, a wolf howled a danger signal. I bolted up out of bed in the darkness. I recognized that howl—it was Junior. Then my phone rang. *Shit.* Fumbling for my cell phone, I jumped up. "Yeah, Beth… what do you need?"

"We've got incoming at the mine. Can you help with the perimeter?" she asked as I heard a car door slam and an engine start.

"Yeah," I said, shaking my head. I quickly dressed and ran

down the stairs. Maggie was still sleeping. She should be good until morning when Nurse Hatch arrived.

Throwing open the back door, I shifted, barely having time to pull the door close behind me before my hand turned to a paw. I broke into a run, my paws hitting the pavement, propelling me through downtown in a flash of silver fur.

I caught sight of two brand new white Jeeps roaring around the corner, headed for the mines, both with Potentia Security on the side.

The larger one was driven by Easton, who was driving with the window down. He caught sight of me and lifted his hand before power sliding around the corner. Kind of impressive driving for the white Jeep Wagoneer. I suspected they had Buster at Mt. Strom Motors put some aftermarket parts in.

Beth's smaller Jeep Renegade followed, doing an equally impressive slide. The team was going in, which meant we needed to patrol the mountainside to make sure no demons snuck out.

Lifting my muzzle, I howled for the pack. It was a familiar howl that meant, "Join us and get paid." As this had been a lean month, I knew we would have a good turnout.

Instead of taking the road to the mine, I slipped into the woods, heading for our meet-up location. More howls joined the night as I raced through dark green underbrush, night smells overwhelming my senses.

Breaking into the clearing, I found a dozen wolves, all in some variation of silver and black. My four brothers were there, along with the male head of every family unit. My sister was missing, but she had a pass. "Let's go. Mountainside," I howled, barely slowing down.

Junior clamored to run beside me, keeping up easily to my left. "Took you long enough," he yipped at me.

"Quiet!" I barked as we headed up toward the mine entrance.

Randy joined me on my right, with my other brothers, Frankie and Dennis, trailing behind with the rest of the pack.

The entire mine site was covered with a chain-link fence, which kept the teenagers and urban explorers out. But about a mile up the slope, where it got steep, the razor wire at the top disappeared. No human could make it up there on foot. It was strenuous enough for us. And luckily, we knew of a spot where the fence was easy to slip through under the bottom.

We headed straight there and scaled the steep hill, panting with exertion.

Making it to the fence, we slipped through, one by one. I turned to Junior. "Let's split into two groups. You take the lower mountains, and I'll lead the top."

Junior yipped in agreement and split off, with Randy and a few others going with him.

I was glad to have Frankie and Dennis with me—friendly faces I could trust. Although I realized, in the back of my head, we had been splitting up like this more and more lately.

But this was no time for pack politics. We had work to do. As expected, when we reached one of the side tunnels, there were already a few demons who had found their way to the surface.

These demons from hell were insectoid, with dark red skin, gigantic eyes, and all teeth and fangs. They were also not the brightest things and always attacked us instead of running.

The problem, at least for them, was that we were pure hard muscles. Werewolves are pure killing power—our skin is thick and immune to their teeth and claws.

I reached the first one and snatched it by its neck. It made a weird squealing noise as I whipped my head back and forth, snapping its spine with a satisfying crack.

I let the body drop out of my mouth just as another one jumped at my back, trying to bite me. It got only a mouthful of silver fur as Frankie growled and jumped. He got the demon off my back, but I stumbled and rolled.

I slid down the mountainside in a hail of dust and rocks, coming to a rest about twenty feet down. Now the demons were running down the hill toward me.

We were the only thing that stood between these demons and the town. Well, us and a flimsy chain-link fence. The fence wasn't much of a deterrent, to be honest.

But we already had the upper hand. While I handled the demons who reached me first, the rest of the pack picked them off from the group. Within minutes, we'd dispatched them all.

As was usual with demons, once dead, they faded away, headed back to hell where they would regroup and come again… as long as the portal remained open.

I hoped Beth and her crew were working on getting that closed as soon as possible.

With that hot spot taken care of, we looped around to the back side of the mountain. Rocky tailing piles and forgotten ventilation headframes littered the mountainside. Their rusting structures reached up into the night sky while the battle raged below us in the tunnels. I could hear ghastly noises from below, echoing up from the headframes.

The ventilation shafts back here were dangerous, and today was no exception. As I ran through the rocky paths toward one of the unsecured exit points, something dark jumped from the top, hitting me so hard on the back that it knocked the air out of me.

I was dazed, and the demon clawed at me, shrieking inhumanly. Its claws were tearing into my fur, and it was flying, but it wasn't doing much damage besides being a huge inconvenience.

My brothers were busy fighting, but I caught my breath and shook the demon off. It flew into a series of pipes, then it stopped thrashing. It had landed on top of one, which pierced its body.

A howl alerted me and I turned toward it. In alarm, I saw a named demon slipping out. Instantly, I knew who it was, our biggest problem—Sarah.

Sarah was human once and a neighbor here in town. In fact, I knew her, years ago, before she turned into a minion of hell. In her youth, she had been a hot, young, vivacious girl who loved to party. Blond hair, blue eyes, pretty enough to model. I have to admit, I may have had a tiny crush on her.

But she wasn't a good person. Eventually, she caught the eye of the town Lutheran Priest, Clay Allard. They married and had a few kids. At that point, I was long-haul truck driving, but I heard it didn't end well. They divorced and she ran off north with her twin girls.

It was years later when she returned, this time, a dentist on her arm. Ironically, Beth Potentia's ex-husband. By that time, she was already twisted by the devil himself, and she tried to get to Beth. Actually, tried to kill her a couple of times before she died in a hail of bullets.

Now, some people might be glad the madwoman who was trying to kill them was dead. You might think, "Well, now I don't have to watch my back anymore." But the problem is, Sarah was an agent of the devil. When she died, she went straight downstairs, where her new boss happily made her a named demon, granting her special powers.

It had been a few years since this happened, and in the few times I had seen her since she took up her new calling, she had changed. It was happening a little at a time. Now, she was over six feet tall, red-skinned with long red nails, a twisted face, and wild blond hair rising above her head. She wore a bright red party dress, hanging in tatters.

She turned to me as if daring me to chase her. Fire danced now on her fingers. She smiled and twisted her fingers in the air, mocking me to come closer.

"Oh, little puppy. Come play," she taunted. Her face twisted, and then she turned and ran toward the fence.

"Get her!" I roared, and my pack stopped immediately, shaking off demons. We took off with a collective howl.

She had a head start, and she was faster than I remembered. When she reached the fence, she scrambled up in one leap, her hand grabbing the top, and then she vaulted over.

"Run, run as fast as you can, you can't catch me!" she jeered before deliberately stomping her foot, causing a minor rockslide that took her quickly down the hill.

Looking up, I caught the sight of four ravens. That would be the vampires.

They swirled down, watching her. At the bottom of the hill, she ran as fast as she could into the brush, where she disappeared.

My pack mates were finishing the last of the demons. I howled again, "Finish and follow," was the command, and we all headed down to the lower hills to meet up with the rest of the pack.

We would circle around the mountain and the surrounding forests all night until we got the all-clear from Beth. I would let her know Sarah slipped away from us, and I hoped the vampire ravens could track her. She was dangerous, that one.

CHAPTER 6
FATHER BURKE

was exhausted after our night of chasing demons. The operation had been called off at dawn, and we met Beth at the mine entrance. Her team of Easton, Dallas, Father Burke, and Beau were soot-covered and exhausted. Father Burke loaded his power washer, which shot holy water at the demons, into the back of the Jeep before opening the door and sitting inside with a deep sigh.

"Thanks for your help, Sam," Beth said, standing by her open car door. "I know things are tight right now. If you come to the big house, I'll get Tina to cut you a check right away."

I looked over at my four brothers, their eyes were fixed on me, hungry for money. "Of course," I said, then glanced over at Dennis. "Could you stop in and check on Maggie for me? Just make sure the nurse arrives."

"Sure, no problem. Frankie and I will stop by before we open the shop today."

"Thank you!" I said and noticed Junior and Randy exchange a glare.

Junior spoke up, "Randy and I are leaving this afternoon for that business trip. We'll get a little nap, load up the cargo, and then head off," he said, his eyes shifty and avoiding Beth, whose husband was the police chief in this small town.

"Yeah. You going to be gone a few days?" I asked, curiosity piqued. They were acting odd.

"We'll be back next week," Randy volunteered.

"Next week! Why so long?" I asked, my eyes flashing. I needed them for patrol duty while Beth was traveling to the White House.

"We've got a few things to take care of," Randy said, not looking me in the eye.

Beth listened intently, then turned to me. "Tonight was a doozy. Two named ones. Garret and Jesus tracked Sarah into the forest but she gave them the slip. We'll have to keep an eye on the terminals."

"Don't worry about it. I'll ask some elders to join us," I said, biting my lip. I liked to keep the elders out of it—women like my mom, who were more than happy to take care of everything else that needed to be done around the property—but in times of need, I could count on them.

Beth got into her Jeep, nodding in approval. She put the key into the ignition as I said, "I like the new rides, by the way. What did you do with your dad's old Wagoneer? That thing might have been older than me."

She laughed, "Well, after Sarah totaled my old Jeep, I needed a new one. Got a new deal on two Jeeps from Buster. But Dad refused to let me donate the old Jeep Wagoneer to a museum. He's got it under a tarp in the barn."

"That sounds like Oren," I chuckled. Her dad was a hoot. He had run Potentia Security for over thirty years. Now that he was retired, he spent a lot of time on cruises. He said it gave him peace of mind. He didn't have to worry about hell portals on

MIDLIFE MOUNTAIN MOONSHINE 47

boats. I think the old man had some serious PTSD, but who was I to judge?

I checked my phone quickly, sending a text to Maggie to let her know my brothers would be stopping by, and then shifted into my wolf form.

The pack quickly followed and we ran together just off the road that led to the mine. As it was daylight, we would be more careful not to be spotted. One wolf didn't cause much alarm around here, but a pack of 'em was enough to get people worried.

Just outside of town, we split up, the pack headed to Silverthorn land. I took off west toward the big house, swinging around town and sneaking out of the woods and across dirt roads when there were no cars to avoid getting spotted.

Finally, I reached the gate to the road of the big house. Looking up, I saw a lone raven just circling down. That would be Garret.

I shifted and walked the rest of the drive on two feet instead of four, reaching the porch just as Garret landed.

I waited for him to shift, watching him turn purple and ripple as he changed. The transformation complete, a grinning vampire stood in front of me.

Today, Garret was wearing a black hoodie and jeans. He pulled up the hood and stepped into the shadows. "Sam. How's my favorite werewolf? I saw you kicking demon butt today from above. Impressive."

"Hi, Garret!" I said, giving him a grin. "I talked to Jesus last night. Seems like decades ago. I need a nap."

A flash of annoyance crossed his face. "Was he bugging you? He likes the ladies. I don't claim him… his coven just happens to be in the holler. We find it a beneficial working relationship. They are contractors, just like you."

"I know. I saw them with you earlier. He warned me about something he thinks my brothers are up to."

"Oh, you mean the drugs?" Garret said, a smirk on his lips. His skin was pale and his dark eyes danced with laughter.

"Drugs? Right. Why does everyone know what my brothers are up to?" I sighed, running a hand through my hair. "I really don't need these problems right now. With Maggie being sick and all…"

"How is she?" he asked, his grin falling. "I've always liked Maggie. Hey, listen. Maybe I could change her…"

"Into a vampire?" I was horrified. "I appreciate the offer, but I can't imagine being married to a vampire. Could you imagine?"

"Yeah, I could," he laughed, and then his smile dropped. "But I'm forever alone."

"Listen, don't spread this around, but I'm going to change her into a werewolf. I'm told it will cure the cancer."

Garret's eyebrows raised. "Oh, I didn't realize you could change people too. Guess I should have remembered my history lessons."

"Well," I shrugged. "We are all busy. But do you want to come to my wedding?"

"Wedding? What's this about a wee little wedding? Why haven't I been asked to do the honors?" I heard a cheerful Irish man say from behind me, and saw Father Burke coming out of the barn, followed by Easton.

Beau and Dallas Drake, the resident shape-shifting dragons, pulled out of the barn in a Ford F150 pickup truck. They drove past, waving goodbye. I was sorry I hadn't seen them in action today. It was always a delight to see two dragons light up the sky. They could exterminate a few hundred demons at a time with their fire.

"Father Burke, hi," I said with a smile. He truly was a treasure sent straight from Rome. He was the predominant exorcist in the world, and not too bad a shot with a holy water pressure washer. "Maggie and I are getting married. It's going to have to be a small little thing at the courthouse. The Lutheran Priest won't marry us."

"Because you're gay?" Father Burke said, a note of horror in his voice. "What a bigoted fool. I'll have to have words with Pastor Etherridge. I didn't know he felt that way, the Lutherans being so liberal and all."

'No, actually. That wasn't the problem. He wouldn't do it because I'm a werewolf. Lord only knows what he would have said if I told him I plan to change Maggie."

Father Burke's eyes lit up. "Perfect! That will cure her of cancer, won't it? Normally, I wouldn't approve of turning a person into a werewolf, it being a permanent condition and all, but she's so sick, it would be a blessing, wouldn't it?"

"It would. I'm just a little worried…" I trailed off, thinking of the process.

"Well, I'll say a prayer. Say, what if I married you two?" Father Burke suggested, clapping his big Irish hand on my shoulder.

My mouth dropped. "But… but you're Catholic."

"Yeah, so what? What's the pope going to do, excommunicate me?" He laughed. "I don't care what the church says about gay marriage. They can go kick rocks. What they don't know won't hurt 'em, will it?"

I threw back my head and laughed, then wiped away tears. "I would be honored if you would marry us." I looked around at the crew, all listening intently. "It would be a small thing, just friends and family. We won't do it until Beth gets back from her trip. Sounds like I'm going to have a busy week."

"Aye. Lovely. I'll pencil you in between fighting pretty demons and doing a bit o' exorcism. I can easily say a few brief words over two lovely lassies," Father Burke said. He jumped up the steps and did a bit of a jig. "It will be fun. Can't wait to see Gregory's face when I tell him what I've done," he laughed heartedly, talking about his best friend, who was the pope. I guess it was good to have the pope as your best friend... you get to break all the rules.

I smiled and followed him inside. I had a much-needed check to pick up.

CHAPTER 7
THE COVEN

I wasn't going for a big wedding, but when my mamma heard Maggie and I were planning to marry, she put her foot down. Originally, I planned a tiny little ceremony in the front room of the salon, but she had her own ideas.

"Listen, you are the leader of this pack. That means your wedding is a public event, and the entire pack has to come," my mom said firmly over the phone.

"Mom," I protested. "Maggie's not up for a big party, and to be honest, I've never been a crafty gal. That's Katie, remember? I haven't got time to order flowers or plan out a big dinner. Heck, we don't even have money to pay for a big shindig."

"Baby girl," she said with a sigh. I could practically feel her stomping her foot from here. Maggie looked over at me. I was sitting on the little cot next to her with a bunch of paperwork spread out.

I was really trying to get a handle on these bills. If Maggie wasn't going to die, that meant no life insurance and no financial relief. I didn't care about the money, to be honest, but it looked like we were going to have to find a house up on Silverthorn land to live in. All the ones available were vacant for reasons. They had more holes in the roofs and baseboards than a cheese grater and were occupied by armies of field mice.

"What?" I said, my voice brimming with trapped energy. Maggie smiled as she watched me talk.

"You don't worry about a thing. You just show up. I'll work it out with Father Burke. Give me his number, please."

I sighed and gave her his cell phone number. I wondered how he would take being called by my mother, the queen of bossiness. She hung up and I knew she would soon get busy planning. That's what a pack Luna did, plan out all the social events. Soon, the responsibility and the title would fall to Maggie.

"So that's it. In a few days, we will be married," Maggie said with a smile. "And then you can change me."

I got up and sat by her, taking her hand. I leaned over and kissed her gently and then smoothed back her brown hair. Her eyes were full of love, which made what I was about to do ten times worse.

Closing my eyes, I moved her hand up to my mouth, and before I changed my mind, I shifted.

Maggie let out a little shriek as I changed. I could feel my wolf's weight on the bed. I was sitting on my haunches. Instinctively, my front paws pushed her down, but gently.

If she struggled, I would have stopped immediately, but she knew what I was doing. "Be gentle," she said, her left hand reaching up to stroke my neck.

Ever so gently, I nipped the fatty part of her upper arm, feeling my teeth sink into her skin, and the taste of her salty blood filled my mouth. I instantly released her and then jumped down off the bed, shifting back as fast as I could into my human form.

"Dang, that stings," Maggie said, grinning at me as she held her arm. "Although, that was a cheap trick. You should have told me you were going to do it now. You're cute as a wolf by the way."

I ran my hand through my silver hair, looking at her nervously. Reaching down, I pulled out a first aid kit, which I had tucked away this morning.

"I'm sorry. Now is the perfect time, and I was afraid I would chicken out." I wrapped her arm but didn't clean out the wound. We needed my wolf germs to do their work.

Fishing out her morning pills from their orange bottles, I lined them up in little cups. "Just think, in a few days, you won't need all this."

"That's a nice thought," she said, popping pill after pill and then taking a drink of water. "I feel weird already. Tired."

"Rest up. Nurse Clara should be here soon, and then I have to run over to the holler." I went to the sink and washed my mouth out. Relief filled me as I realized I didn't like the taste of blood. I guess I didn't need to worry about turning into a man-eating werewolf.

When I turned around, Maggie was already sleeping, her hair spread out on the pillow. If my calculations were correct, she would change the morning of our wedding. Then, I could introduce her to the pack.

There was a knock on the door, and Nurse Hatch came bustling in, her bag clanking suspiciously. It sure sounded like she had the two quarts of moonshine I gave her for working late in her purse.

"Good morning," she said, smelling strongly of booze. I tilted my head and looked at her. She was clearly hungover.

"You have any of that moonshine left? Or have you gone through it already?" I asked with a raised eyebrow.

"I don't know why it's any of YOUR concern," she said, putting her purse down on the counter near the front door.

"You seem to have a problem with drinking. And you're right, I don't care what you do in your spare time." I shrugged, feeling bad about being the one to provide her with the very thing that was destroying her life.

She sighed. "Well, yeah. I guess it's not a big secret. I show up to work every day, and I'm mostly sober."

I nodded. "Maggie's had her meds already this morning. She might be running a little fever today. I'm going to stay with her tomorrow, just in case."

"Just in case of what?" Nurse Hatch asked, picking up her book and settling in on one of the customer couches in the front room. This was where she usually spent her days while Maggie was sleeping.

I didn't have the heart to tell her that Maggie might turn into a werewolf tomorrow and eat her, so I shrugged. "And I'm not sure we will need you next week. Or any time after that, in fact."

She froze, looking like a deer in headlights. "Oh, dear, so little time left? Maggie has been a perfect gem to work with. I'm sorry this is happening so soon."

Clearly, she thought Maggie was on her deathbed. I didn't have the heart to tell her that she was going to be cured effectively in two days. "I'll give you a good reference and won't mention the drinking on the job."

Nurse Hatch blinked her eyes, looking shocked that I would even accuse her of such a thing. "I only drink after hours!"

"Listen, I wasn't born yesterday, but seriously, consider some AA meetings or something," I said, shoving my phone into my back pocket. My flannel jacket hung by the door, and I grabbed it on my way out. I had some vampires to visit.

I went on foot, running through the forest the few miles to the holler. Really, the holler was part of Mt. Storm, but it was set down in a small valley with just one road winding into it. Wooden shacks appeared, changing to trailers just up the road. Farther down was a small neighborhood of modest ranch homes, their well-maintained exteriors a stark difference to the homes just a few streets away.

Mostly older adults and the working poor lived in this part, with cars up on blocks and trailers with rust on them. Dogs lounged in the shade, lazily chewing old bones.

Beau and Dallas Drake both lived with their families, the shape-shifting dragons, in the nicer part of the neighborhood, but they were not who I was here for. I was looking for Jesus Armando and his coven.

Garret had given me the address and promised he would meet me here. I slipped out of the tree line, spotting him at the top of an old oak tree, on a branch that looked half dead.

He flew down in a rustle of black feathers, shifting into his vampire form in the shadows of the tree. He raised his hand in greeting as he lifted his hood and put on a pair of black glasses.

"Garret. Thanks for coming with me," I said, noting that he was dressed head to toe in black, in a jacket, jeans, and a hoodie, even on this hot fall day.

"Well, one does not just walk into a vampire coven uninvited," Garret said. "Especially not a werewolf. I told them you were coming."

We walked together across the grass and into the trailer park. We arrived at a blue trailer with red roses planted along the front window. This made me giggle, thinking of vampires gardening.

Garret knocked on the door, a series of three sharp raps, and then opened the screen door and stepped inside.

Curiosity got the better of me, and I craned my neck to look around him, anxious to see what a vampire lair looked like.

I shouldn't have been surprised to see that it looked like a typical bachelor pad. A black leather sectional couch took up most of the front room, and the wall was covered with a television screen. A basketball game was on, and the loud sound of sneakers on the floor made me wince.

Jesus was sitting with an older woman, who was wearing a leather corset, a net skirt, and had on the reddest lipstick I'd ever seen.

I couldn't help but notice bite marks on her neck as Jesus took his arm off her shoulder and looked at us coldly.

"Hola, Garret. You've brought a friend today," Jesus said nonchalantly as the woman got up, glanced at us without saying a word, and went down the hall.

"I'll be waiting for you," she said, licking her lips and opening a door, which I assumed led to his bedroom.

"Sorry to interrupt… ahhh, lunchtime," Garret said, glancing toward the woman.

"No worries, mi amigo. What can I do for you?" Jesus fixed his gaze on me, gesturing for us to join him on the couch. He picked up the television remote and turned the basketball game down.

A blond vampire came out of the bedroom on the right. I had seen him around the holler and knew his name was Paul. He always carried a skateboard and wore his long hair down over his eyes.

He wore baggy shorts with an Orlando Magic cap on backwards, which allowed me to see his startling blue eyes. He wasn't wearing a shirt, and his chest looked like something out of a weightlifting magazine. He seemed pissed as he went into the kitchen and pulled out a blood bag from the fridge. He bit into it ferociously, emptying it in seconds. He threw the bag in the trash and then noticed I was watching him. His eyes widened in surprise and his nostrils flared.

"Boss. Why did you invite a freaking werewolf into our house?" he asked, clearly irritated at my presence.

Jesus shrugged. "Garret brought her."

"This isn't a dog-friendly house," Paul snapped, his hands closing into fists.

I gave him a lopsided smile. "Listen, I get it. You don't like my kind. But I'm hoping we can work together."

Paul glanced over at Jesus and shrugged. "I'll work with you if the boss says so, but I won't be happy about it."

Garret's face was expressionless, but he sat back and I could feel his black eyes sizing me up. "We kind of already do work together. Indirectly."

"Listen, I need help with a personal problem. You said the other night my brothers were working for the cartels. I'm not happy about that."

Jesus nodded, glancing back toward his room. "I don't like to get Justina involved. You understand, messing with the cartels is dangerous. Your brothers are playing with el fuego."

"Fire." I laughed. "The one thing that can hurt us. What do you know?"

"It started a few months ago. Your oldest brother, the one that sells moonshine, has always come to the holler. I guess these people here are your biggest customers. I find it odd you would take advantage of your neighbors, but who am I to judge?"

My hackles rose as anger filled me and I went on the defense. "Listen, the Silverthorns have been selling shine for generations. I don't love it, to be honest, but I don't see any way to bring it to a stop. My family lives off that money. What do *you* do to support your family?"

Jesus chuckled, "I'm not sure you really want to know, Sam. But let's just say it involves consenting adults and a pay-per-view website."

My mouth dropped open. "Really?"

"Really," he said with a smile. "It's all completely above board. I assure you."

I shook my head, "Okay, then. Ummm, what brought Junior to your attention?"

"When we are not busy, my friends and I like to look after the people here. Too many drugs coming in and out. The cartels got scared of us, which was good. You might have read some stories about hikers found dead in the State Park. Those weren't all hikers."

"Vigilante vampires. Okay," I said with a shrug. "Who am I to judge?"

"Exactly. We ran out a lot of the crime. But I've seen your brother around, and he's not just selling moonshine... he's got brown-wrapped packages."

"So, why didn't you stop him?" I asked, shifting in my seat.

"I didn't want to start a war with the Silverthorns." Jesus looked at me with that same dead gaze. "But I could ask *you* why you can't control your pack."

"Well, I-I." The words were stuck on my tongue. "My brothers, Junior, and Randy have always been a thorn in my side. It's a bit of a power struggle, really. I have to let them do what they want to do or they may try to take over the pack."

Jesus's eyes narrowed. "Well, I can't stop him. I did approach him, and we almost got into a physical fight. He threatened to tear my head off. I like it on my shoulders."

I sighed, thinking that a fight between my brothers and this coven of vampires wouldn't end well for anyone. One of us or them would get killed.

"My friends and I took it upon ourselves to follow them. We caught them at the quarry, just outside Kessel. They met up with a group of tough-looking werewolves. Packages and cash were exchanged."

My mouth dropped open. "Are you telling me the cartel have other werewolves?"

"Appears so. No idea where they are from, though." He rubbed his chin, and then yelled down the hall. "Paul! Come here."

Paul popped out of his room again and ambled down the hall. He had changed into a hoodie and a pair of baggy jeans. His hat was on the right way around now, and he wore a pair of dark, wraparound sunglasses. "Whatcha need, boss? I was just going to head out to the corner and keep watch."

Jesus nodded. "I was telling Sam here about her brother... the one we caught red-handed."

"Perro," Paul spat, his eyes narrowing, and then he brushed his bangs away, looking at me suspiciously.

"Don't worry, I know who my brother is." I shrugged. "If I can, I'll put a stop to it."

"That didn't sound very convincing," Garret injected, putting a hand on my arm. "You sure you can handle it?"

"I'm going to have to, aren't I? You got any more information on this? Does he meet at a certain time at this quarry?"

"Every Thursday afternoon, it seems," Garret said.

I turned to him. "How do you know?"

He hesitated for a moment. "If you must know, I've joined Jesus's coven. I would appreciate it if you didn't mention it to Beth. I don't know that she would like me moonlighting, so to speak."

I just stared at him in shock. For years, Garret had been the Potentia Security resident vampire. Heck, he even lived on the grounds in a little shack behind the big house.

"Today is Thursday." My mind was spinning. "Junior and Randy are supposed to be leaving for Maine today."

Garret smiled, "Well, I think Kessel is on the way to Maine, isn't it?"

"I wonder who these werewolves are. Are they the Kentucky Caines?" I asked, naming off a few of the closer packs. "Or maybe the Tennessee Novas?"

"No idea, but maybe you should find out." Jesus shrugged.

"Good idea. Anyone want to come with me?"

"I'm in," Paul said, pushing up his glasses and pulling up his hood.

The door to the other bedroom opened, and the third vampire of this coven came out—a Hispanic vampire named Carlos. He was in the middle of putting on his own hoodie. "I'm in," he said.

"Were you listening?" Garret asked with a slow smile.

"Of course," Carlos said. "I had my ear pressed up to the door the entire time."

"Well, let me tell Justina we won't be making that video this afternoon. Looks like we are all going," Jesus said, getting up off the couch and calling down the hall.

"Justina! We are going out! Don't wait for me, dear one."

She opened the door with a pout. "Always working, Jesus.

I'm going to get carry out, then. You ate, but I haven't had anything."

"No problemo," Jesus said, fishing out his wallet and handing her a twenty. "We'll be back later."

"Have fun," she said, taking the money and delicately tucking it into the top of her corset. "But not too much fun. I've got plans for you later."

CHAPTER 8
THE QUARRY

As none of the vampires owned a car, we took my truck. Garret sat shotgun, and the three other vampires changed into ravens and flew overhead.

Garret pulled his hood lower and slouched down, shoving his hands deep into the front pouch of the hoodie. "It's hot as hell in here. Don't you have AC?" he complained.

"No, sorry. It's broken." I shrugged and rolled down the window.

He shook his head and rolled down his side. "Too bright today," he said, flipping down the sun visor. "I should be at home in my nice, dark little cabin. But no, somehow, I got roped into this little adventure."

"Why did you join Jesus's coven?" I asked. "I always thought of you as a loner."

He chuckled, "Believe it or not, my counselor suggested it."

"Counselor? You see a counselor?" I said, flabbergasted. A vampire seeking mental health advice was unique to say the least. I wonder if he told her about his "condition." I know I certainly wouldn't be able to unload my paranormal existence problems to someone with no clue.

He laughed. "Yeah. I find therapy helpful. I determined I was lonely, and she suggested I find a group of like-minded people to join. I didn't tell her I was a vampire, of course."

"Well, good for you," I said. "It's so important to have people who understand."

He didn't comment, and instead reached over to turn on my radio. The knob came off in his hand. "Your truck is, as Jesus would say, caca."

"Listen, I know it's shit. But it's the only wheels I've got," I said. "It's either drive this or the van we use for deliveries. Actually, that's probably going to be what my brothers are driving right now. Keep an eye out."

It was only about a thirty-minute drive to Kessel, and while driving, I pulled out my cell phone and dialed Junior's number. He picked up on the first ring. "Hey, just checking in to make sure you left this morning," I said, passing a semi-truck. The wind blew through the cabin, keeping it moderately comfortable.

"Yeah, we're on the road," he said, his voice clipped. "I can hear you're driving."

"Headed to Winchester to take Maggie to the doctors." The lie flowed smoothly off my tongue.

"Okay then. Well, I'm getting ready to stop for a minute to take a piss. But I'll be back on the road in no time. We should have this load taken care of by Friday, and I'll be back in time for your little wedding Mom has planned," he said, his voice showing no emotion.

"Great! Glad you are coming. I didn't plan for it to be that big, but Mom insisted," I said. Garret looked over at me, and then shifted into a raven in a flash of purple, flying straight out of the window and up into the sky to join the others. The sun must have gotten to him.

"She told me I had to come," he said, disdain in his voice. I felt a moment of anger. Of course, Mom had to demand he come. Junior never liked Maggie, or the fact that I was gay.

"Well, I'll see you soon," I said, and he grunted before hanging up the phone. *What an ass.*

I only drove a few more minutes before Garret came back. He shifted, leaving a pile of dark feathers on my seat, which immediately flew through the air, causing me to sneeze.

"Sorry." He shrugged. "You're going to want to pull off at this rest stop. Park near the back," he said as I quickly took the next exit.

"You're supposed to signal," he said as a truck honked at me.

"Yeah, well, the signal flasher is broken," I said. "And I haven't had time to take this into my brother's shop." I parked near the back of the rest stop, well away from the pit toilets and the truck drivers. The ravens flew down, landing near the tree line.

Jesus shifted, his black feathers flying through the air. He perched on the tree limb, his feet under him, his hands on the trunk. He pointed off in the distance. "The quarry is about a mile away, through these trees. It looks like your brother is already there, waiting for the others to show up."

"I want to get an eye on those werewolves. I wonder if they are coming by foot?" I said while scanning the parking lot. I didn't see anything that looked suspicious, but then, in the trees, I heard a wolf howl.

Instantly, my hackles rose. That wasn't any werewolf I knew. I casually strolled over to the trees, stepping into the shade. Jesus quickly shifted back to his bird form and then the four ravens sat on the oak tree limb, all in a row, their black beady eyes staring at me. "Let's go. Stay up overhead and back me up."

The ravens all bobbed their heads in unison and I dropped to all fours, feeling my werewolf power flow through me as I shifted. My fur grew over me and my senses sharpened. I was upwind from the werewolves. There was more than one, and I instantly knew who it was.

It's the King Clan. I don't understand, I thought to myself. *They are our allies.*

I picked up the pace, following the scent through the forest. Thankfully, the wind was blowing in my favor. I reached a chain-link fence and looked out of the bushes. The now-flooded remnants of the limestone quarry stretched out in front of me, glimmering in the sun. The fresh scent of water filled my senses, and I licked my lips, longing to lap a few mouthfuls.

Ducks settled onto the lake water, which was an idyllic scene, but across the water, I could make out the white van with its rear doors open. A bright yellow moving van sat next to it with the ramp down.

A raven landed in front of me and shifted, and this time, it was Garret—his face unreadable behind the sunglasses. "They are busy exchanging cargos. Looks like just two men. I think they are werewolves like you… they stink to high heaven," Garret said.

"I'm going to pay my brothers a little unexpected visit. You all hang back," I said, as Garret shifted and then flew up and joined the other three ravens overhead.

I wasn't sure this was a good idea, but I was out of options. I would play it cool and pretend like I knew what the hell was going on.

Running around the shore of the lake, I felt the breeze on my face. My eyes were intent on the two men who looked familiar, and Randy and Junior. Their backs were to me as they worked.

I was about fifty feet away before they noticed me. Junior froze, a box in his hands. "Shit! Sam. What the hell are you doing here? I thought you were taking Maggie to Winchester."

The two King Clan werewolves, looked up from the bottles they were transferring, and I was shocked when one took a gun out, which had been tucked into the small of his back. As I got closer, I recognized the two wolves. Silas and Logan King. We had met, years back. "What are you doing here?" Silas King said, his voice rising.

I shifted, feeling four sets of eyes on me, and then I held out my hand. "Thought I would come out and see what the boys were up to. I didn't know the King pack would send it's leaders to do a simple hand off." A smile was plastered on my face.

Silas shoved the gun back into his waistband and smiled back. "Oh, hey… sorry about the gun. You can't be too careful with this cargo. It's been awhile. Last I recall we were here for Jonas' wedding."

I grinned, keeping it neutral. "That was a long time ago."

Logan put down a box and crossed his arms across his chest. "Don't see much of our little brother anymore. Should have sent him out to meet us."

"I didn't know you were coming, or we could have had a little reunion. I thought these two were driving to Maine. Umm, can I ask you all what you are doing?" I glanced over at my own brothers, who looked guilty as hell, their eyes downturned and their hands shoved in their pockets.

"You don't know?" Silas said, cocking his head and looking at me. "These two told me you were on board."

"Junior, you going rogue on your sister?" Logan said,

leaning up against the moving van. He was looking at me carefully, his reddish-brown hair glinting in the sun. Logan was built like the van he was standing against, tough and sturdy, and I certainly wouldn't want to meet him in a fight.

I was acutely aware it was four against little old me, but I glanced up to see my raven friends circling above. "I've been busy lately. You all want to clue me in?"

"Well, you know, sis. We had this moonshine to sell. The Kings agreed to sell it to us, but it's more of a swap, you see. They had some product to move, so we are going to do a bit of a switcheroo. A trade deal, so to speak."

I looked at the black tote box, and then over at the crates of moonshine. "How long has this deal been going on?"

"Well, we've been trading for about a year now," Junior said, running a hand through his silver and black hair. "Jonas didn't tell you?"

Randy had taken his vape out and was blowing clouds of vapor in my direction. "You have a problem, sis?"

I glanced over at the Kings. "I'm sorry, but we can't take this shipment today."

"What?" Silas said, his face going hard. He glanced over at my brothers, "We had a deal. My partners expect to be paid."

"We do have a deal. Sam, get out of here. We can talk about this later," Junior said, his jaw clenching. Randy moved closer to me with both fists tightened, and I took a step back.

"Looks like it's four against one, little lady," Silas drawled, his eyes fixing on me, daring me to challenge him. He casually took his gun back out of his waistband, holding it at his side.

Just then, all four ravens dropped down, shifting into their human forms in midair. I heard the thump of their shoes as they hit the ground next to me. Jesus grinned, his fangs bright white in the sunlight. He lifted his arms, cartoon-like, towards the Kings.

Junior's mouth dropped. "You brought the stinking vampires with you? What the hell, Sam? Looks like an entire coven."

I crossed my arms. "Listen, I don't want trouble. What's going to happen is that the Kings are going to go back to Maine with this cargo, and we will go back to Mt. Storm with our cargo. I'll handle my brothers. I'm sorry you had to drive all this way for a deal they didn't clear with me first."

Silas drew back his gun and looked at it thoughtfully. "I should have brought the silver bullets. Didn't think I would need them today."

"We don't want no problemo," Jesus said, pushing his glasses back on his face. "Our amiga here asked us for help. She's a good friend."

I thought that was taking it a bit far as I'd just met the coven this morning, but since I considered Garret a friend, I let it slide.

"A Spanish vampire. Great. What are you doing here? Do you even have a green card?" Silas said dismissively.

Jesus and Carlos looked at each other, and then at Silas.

"You shouldn't have said that," Paul said, shaking his blond head. "Jesus and Carlos were both born here in the States. They don't like it when people make assumptions."

"Boys!" I yelled, raising my hand. The tension was thick in the air. "Let's go our separate ways and call it a day."

Silas stared at me for a moment, and then looked over at Junior. "This isn't over. You owe me." He jerked his head towards his brother, and Logan looked at the back of the truck.

"What about what we've already loaded?" he asked, I had caught them about halfway in between switching the cargo.

"If you are all agreeable, let's just leave it as it is," I said with a shrug, thinking I would have to somehow get rid of the illegal drugs. Maybe they could be burned or buried when we got back home. This was a blow—a big blow. Half of the moonshine was in the back of their van already, and there was no way I was going to let my brothers sell drugs in the holler.

"Fine. I'm not happy," Silas said, and we watched Logan put the ramp up and then the two brothers got in the truck, slamming the doors shut.

They drove off while I was standing with my brothers, glaring at them. I could feel the vampires behind me and I was happy they were there.

"You made a big mistake, sis," Junior said. "That was half our inventory. But I guess if we sell—"

"No!" I said, cutting him off. "We aren't selling drugs. What is even in those bags?"

"Meth," Randy said, his eyes looking shifty.

"You're poisoning your neighbors," Jesus said, his voice rising and his eyes filled with anger. "And destroying our community."

"Listen, if I didn't provide it, they would get it somewhere else," Randy said, closing the doors of the van.

"What are you going to tell the pack next month, sister, when you have $0 to distribute?"

I paused and licked my lips. "There is still some moonshine left, and you can all make a new batch."

Junior threw back his head and laughed, then he turned to the van. "No, I don't think so. Randy and I are on strike. This will teach you a lesson about interfering with us."

My heart hammered in my chest as I watched them get in the van and pull away. I turned to my vampire friends, my shoulders sagging. "Well, thank you for the back-up."

"Your brothers are bad news," Paul said, watching them turn

and drive out of the quarry with the highly illegal cargo still in the back.

"I would watch my back, Sam," Garret agreed, putting his hand on my shoulder.

I shivered, and not just because his skin was cold. "Let's head back. I need to go and check on Maggie."

CHAPTER 9
THE LAW

We were on US 48 headed west. My brothers were ahead of me in the van, doing 70 in the right lane.

I hadn't really intended to follow them home, but here we were. I'm certain they thought I was making sure they didn't make any side stops.

My stomach growled and I considered pulling off to get a bag of chips at a gas station in Maysville, but I kept on going. There were benefits to keeping the boys in sight. I could eat at home.

But it was just outside Maysville when disaster struck. A dark navy Ford Explorer came blazing up behind me. Instantly, my foot came off the gas and I dropped down below the speed limit.

A flash of a yellow logo whizzed by me, as the big SUV cut between the van and my truck. My heart sank as the good old cherries and berries up top started to flash.

Gripping the steering wheel, I pulled into the left lane, passing my brothers as they slowed down to pull over. I caught

Junior's angry glare as I passed. He made a motion of a phone with his hand, and my hands scrambled to find my cell phone.

He picked up on the first ring.

"Shit. We're in trouble," he said, breathing heavily.

"Don't say anything, Junior. I'll get you a lawyer. Don't worry," I said, sweat breaking out on my forehead. "Maybe it's fine. Maybe he just wants to give you a warning for going slightly over the speed limit."

"Yeah, right," I heard Randy say in the background. "We're screwed big time."

"He's coming up to the van. I'll call you back if I can," Junior said, and the phone went dead.

I somehow made it to the next exit, pulling off in the parking lot of a heavy equipment rental place. My heart was hammering, and my hands were shaky as I dialed my mom.

She answered with a chirpy hello. "We are all ready for the wedding, dear. Potluck is ready, and your Aunt Lacy is making the wedding cake. You and Maggie should get here by noon tomorrow, and the weather looks good."

"That's great, Mom. But we've got a problem. The state police just pulled Junior and Randy over." I realized I had to be careful what I said now, on my cell.

"Oh, noooo!" Mom wailed. "Is it… bad?"

"I think so," I said, panic rising in my chest. "I need Frankie and Dennis to take care of the business."

"The business?" she asked weakly. "What are you talking about?"

I sighed, "Mom, if they aren't there already, I've got a feeling the police are going to show up looking for things… if you get my drift."

"Oh," she said, alarm in her voice. "Yes, let me see what I can do." And then she paused. "Oh no, someone is at the door."

Grimacing, I rubbed my forehead. "I've got to go. I'll call you back."

I instantly ended the call and phoned Dennis. Hopefully, he wasn't still at the shop.

"Yeah, sis. What's up?" Dennis answered in a laid-back voice. I heard country music in the background.

"Where are you?" I asked, my breath short—on the edge of hyperventilation.

"I'm in my backyard, taking care of the chickens," he said. "What's up? You sound frantic."

"Shift now. Hide what needs to be hidden. Junior and Randy just got pulled over, and it's not good."

"Got you, sis," Randy said, and instantly, the phone went silent. That's what I loved about Randy and Dennis. They were loyal and did what I asked without argument.

Taking a few deep breaths, I watched as a raven swooped down out of the sky, landing next to my truck. In a moment, Garret appeared, opening up the door and slouching down in the seat.

"Your brothers just got arrested," he said, shaking his head. "I stayed up above. Your idiot brother, Randy, tried to resist, so he got roughed up a little. They found the drugs."

I squeezed my eyes shut and rested my forehead on the steering wheel. To my surprise, I felt a cold hand squeezing my shoulder. "It's going to be okay," Garret said calmly.

"No. I don't think it is." My voice caught in my throat.

"There go the police," Garret commented, and my head snapped up. I watched as two police cars whipped past us on the interstate, their lights off.

I pulled out my phone again and placed it on the dash, my hands were shaking so bad.

"Oh, shit. Here's a car for you," Garret said, twisting around and looking behind us. I could see the red and blue lights on his face.

Taking a deep breath, I pulled out my driver's license and reached over to get the insurance out of my glove compartment. Thank God I renewed it a few weeks ago. It was one of the things I had let slide. I rolled down the window and waited, watching the police officer walk up behind me, place his hand on my rear fender, and then approach my window.

"License and registration," I heard a familiar voice say. I looked up. It was Dan Comstock with a stern look on his face.

I handed it over, my hands trembling so bad that the papers shook. He took them from me and looked them over. There was a long pause, and then he said, "Sam, you got anything you shouldn't have in this truck?"

"No," I said, my voice sounding hollow.

"Good. Because I would hate to arrest a friend," he warned. "Now, step outside and we'll talk. You too, Garret."

We both stood on the side of the road. Garret had his hands deep in his pockets and his hood pulled up. A state police car pulled up, and the officer and Dan greeted each other curtly. The state police officer asked us both to put our hands on the vehicle and spread our legs.

Miserably, we hastily complied, and they patted us down, finding nothing. Then, the officer searched my truck, top to bottom, finding a few quarters and a discarded Coke can. All the while, Dan stood with us silently, looking off in the distance.

Interestingly, Dan had left his radio on and I could hear some chatter. The state police and the Mt. Storm police were working together, serving a search warrant on Silverthorn property. We said nothing as we listened to the search.

"Are they going to find anything, Sam?" Dan asked quietly as the state police officer was looking under my passenger seat.

I shrugged and said nothing, refusing to meet his eyes.

"They found a bunch of drugs on your brothers. You know anything about that?"

Again, I said nothing. I needed a lawyer—fast. How I was going to pay him was another matter.

Then Dan turned to Garret. "What do you know about all this? Why are you out here? This isn't a Potentia Security job, I checked with Beth."

"I'm staying out of it," Garret said, shaking his head and shoving his hands deep into his hoodie.

Dan sighed as the state police officer finished. The man ambled over to us, "Well, you two are free to go. I'm giving you a ticket for loitering."

I nodded, taking the paper from him wordlessly. "Thank you, officers." Then I got back in my car, looking down at the ticket. *$150 fine, great. Could this day get any better?*

I watched as the cars pulled away and headed west towards Mt. Storm. "If you don't mind, I'm going to fly home. I'm feeling a bit sun-sick," Garret said, rubbing his head.

"Thanks, Garret. For everything."

"No problem. Let me know if you need anything." He shifted into a raven and flew away.

With a sigh, I called Duchamp and Sons attorney at law, the only lawyer in town.

I didn't have time for this nonsense with my brothers. I made it home, spending the drive back doing damage control. I made a verbal agreement with Chad Duchamp to represent my brothers and myself in court. I talked to Dennis and told him I had been pulled over. He couldn't talk for long because he was standing by as the police combed our property, looking for the stills. The police hadn't found them yet, but that didn't mean they wouldn't. The boys didn't have much time to work the magic that hid them.

I hadn't talked to Junior or Randy yet. I assumed they were currently being grilled on our organization. Hopefully, they would keep their mouths closed. I called Jonas King quickly and told him I needed to talk to him in person. He couldn't talk either because police were at his house.

I half expected to find police cars behind Maggie's Clip and Cut, but thankfully, it was quiet. I pulled in and wasn't surprised to find Nurse Hatch waiting for me at the door.

"Maggie has been acting weird all day. Full of energy. I hear you two are getting married tomorrow?" Nurse Hatch said, her eyebrows rising.

"Yeah, we are. It's been a long day. Remember, this is your last day."

"Oh, yes. I was hoping I could get a few more bottles of Silverthorn's best from you."

"I'm sorry. I'm all out, and frankly, we aren't going to have any for a while."

"Really? Where am I supposed to get my hooch?" she asked, her voice rising.

"The liquor store like everyone else." I shrugged, hearing the television on upstairs. "Excuse me, I need to talk to Maggie. It sounds like she's upstairs?"

"Like I said, full of energy. And just so you know… the liquor store charges twice as much for anything drinkable."

Again, I shrugged and watched as Nurse Hatch made her way down the walk. Then, I hurried up the stairs to see how Maggie was doing.

Maggie was burning up with a fever, but she looked happy and more perky than she had in months. She'd actually left her bed, and was upstairs when I came home, sitting on the sofa in the front room with a huge glass of ice water in front of her.

Her face lit up in a smile when she saw me. "Sam! I feel great today! It's like the heat rolling off me is killing the cancer."

I leaned over and gave her a kiss, her forehead blazing under my lips. I sat down by her and said, "There is a complication. My brothers got arrested today with a bunch of illegal drugs and moonshine in the truck."

"Oh no," she said, her eyes going wide. "This is bad, isn't it?"

I nodded, tears coming to my eyes. "Real bad. They had a warrant to search Silverthorn land too, they are out there now."

"Didn't Dan give you a warning this time?" she asked, taking my hand.

I shook my head. "Although, he did pull me over. It was like he was looking out for me. The cops didn't find anything in my truck, of course. But I guess they could have planted something and taken me in."

"Are we still getting married tomorrow?" Maggie asked, her eyes teary.

"Yeah. Come hell or high water," I said with a shaky smile. Just then, my phone rang, and it was a weird number I didn't recognize.

There was a long recording about how this line was being monitored by the Mt. Storm police, and then the line clicked over. "This is Sam Silverthorn," I said, briskly, holding the phone to my ear.

"Sam. It's Junior. I'm at the county jail. You're my one call."

I sighed, rubbing my eyes. "Hey. I called Chad Duchamp. He's going to represent you."

"They are trying to get one of us to flip," he said, his voice low. "I'm worried about Randy."

"Well, don't. Just don't," I said.

"Yeah, right. Well, thanks for getting the lawyer," Junior said.

"He said he would be in tomorrow to talk to you both. This is going to cost us a fortune, Junior. I'm pissed at you both. Why couldn't you just let things ride? No, you had to…" I let my words trail off. This was a recorded line.

"Well, thanks. You talk to Mom?" Junior said, his voice dropping even lower. I could hear the noises of the station behind him.

"Yeah. Tell Randy to use his phone call to talk to her," I said, rubbing my forehead. I was getting a massive headache. I realized I hadn't eaten all day, and if I didn't get my stress levels under control, I might just have a stroke.

"Will do. Thanks, sis," Junior said. "I've gotta go. My time appears to be up."

I closed my eyes and laid still, letting the stress drain out of my body. I felt Maggie curl up to me, laying her head on my shoulder. Absently, I reached up and stroked her very short hair, just now growing back from the chemo.

"I love you, Sam," she said, her feverish skin making me sweat. I didn't care, it was nice.

"I love you too, Maggie." I leaned down and kissed her forehead.

CHAPTER 10
CHANGES

n the middle of the night, Maggie tapped my shoulder.

I woke up with a start from where I had drifted off on the couch. The light cast from the television hit her face and I could see she didn't look well.

In fact, her face was twisting, the bones seeming to move as I watched. "You're changing," I said with excitement, sitting up too fast, causing me to feel dizzy.

"I feel weird," she said, holding her head in both hands.

"Like your stomach is on a roller coaster and you don't quite fit in your skin anymore?" I asked.

She nodded and I reached over and touched her. Her skin was cool, the fever had broken. I took off the bandage from her arm and noticed it was completely healed.

"If I would have known what a shit-show today was going to be, I would have waited to change you, but I guess we are doing this."

"What's happening to me?" she moaned, rocking back and forth.

"Don't fight it. Listen, whatever you do, stay with me, okay?

We'll go hunting." I stood and picked her up, cradling her in my arms.

Even though I was on the cusp of being an infirm old lady, it was easy as she was all of eighty pounds with the weight she had lost while being sick. I took her outside, watching her start to glow purple. I sat her on her feet, keeping one arm around her as I shut the back door behind me.

The crescent moon shone down on us while crickets chirped from near the downspout. The cool scent of grass and fall leaves filled the air. Taking a glance right and left down the alley, I saw it was empty. It must have been about one o'clock in the morning because Mike Dunn hadn't arrived yet to start making the donuts, and he usually showed up at three am.

I put both my hands on her shoulders, looking deep into her eyes. "Don't fight it. Let it happen. I'm here."

She made a low moaning sound, her body spasming from right to left. I held her in my grip and our eyes made contact. They went from fear to trust, and her brain let her body do what it wanted to do.

Her first shifting went slowly, but soon, she was standing on all fours. I sucked in my breath. Maggie was a beautiful wolf. Her coat was a dark chestnut brown, sprinkled with grey around her face. Her eyes were a deep brown, the color of the forest.

I shifted quickly and then raised my nose to the sky, letting out a howl of excitement.

And then, together, we turned and ran through the sleepy streets of Mt. Storm. It was quiet, with just the sound of our running feet and the scuttling of feral cats and night critters who got out of our way.

We looped through the town, and I could tell Maggie was hungry. She tried to jump on a rat, missing as it scurried out of her grasp. I gave a yip that meant, "Don't waste your time," and turned north toward Silverthorn lands.

We ran down the long dirt road that led to home, the moon giving us plenty of light. I howled again, and a few minutes later, we were joined by one wolf, and then another. Soon, nearly half the pack joined us, full of silver coats and curious eyes.

They surrounded Maggie protectively, and when we stopped, they sniffed her up and down and touched noses with her. "Hunt!" I commanded with a sharp bark, then we turned and headed into the trees.

We found the deer quickly. Of course, we did… our noses never failed us. We took it down, biting and tearing through the fur to get at the fresh meat. Maggie ate furiously, and the others stepped aside to let her feast. A new werewolf was always hungry, and it was better to let her eat than to deal with a hangry she-wolf.

With the carcass nearly devoured, we headed back to the campfire at a slow pace, licking our muzzles clean. Settling around the cold fire, we shifted one right after the other, leaving only Maggie in her wolf form.

While my brother, Dennis, started a fire, I went and crouched down next to Maggie. "It's easy to shift back. Just envision yourself in your body. Let go of your wolf spirit, and let the human one come forward."

The purple sputtered around her like a wet brand, and then grew stronger. We all watched as she transformed into the Maggie we all knew and loved. I put my arm around her and kissed her gently to the applause of my family.

We sat by the fire and my mother came by, crouched down, and took her hands, squeezing them gently. "I'm happy you are joining our pack. Even more so because, now, I give up my spot as Luna. It passes to you."

"Luna?" Maggie asked, her brow furrowing.

I took a deep breath and then launched into the simplest explanation I could muster. "I'm the leader. The Alpha. The leader's mate is the Luna. Since I never married, my mother remained the pack Luna."

Maggie looked confused, "If you're the leader, who is your second in command?"

I shrugged. "I never picked a Beta. My brothers would have been jealous. Don't worry, I'll explain all the politics later," I said quietly.

We sat by the fire. This wasn't an official pack meeting, but Dennis explained what had happened earlier.

"I got your call, shifted, and howled for help. We were able to hide the stills. Luckily, they were empty, so we didn't have to take the time to dump anything out. The police didn't find anything," he announced proudly.

I sighed with relief and then looked around the pack. Nearly everyone had joined us now, except Junior and Randy. "You all deserve an explanation. The boys were running more than moonshine. They got caught with drugs and the police took everything. You need to prepare yourselves for hard times."

There were audible gasps. I saw a few furtive looks though, which made me think that it wasn't a complete secret.

"Rhett!" I said, calling out one of my cousins. He was looking at the ground, his face ashen. "Did you know about this?"

Rhett looked up, guilt all over his face. He nodded his head. "I'm sorry. It seemed a good way to bring some cash into the pack. You know, things have been tough. I needed new brakes on my truck, and I was complaining to Junior about how money was so tight. He gave me a few hundred and told me not to tell you. I suspected something was up. I should have come to you."

"Anyone else want to confess?" I asked, looking around the group. Maggie, for her part, sat next to me, her eyes wide and listening.

"Yeah," Lulu, Randy's young wife, said. "I helped the boys sell drugs in the holler. They did it because they wanted to help. They didn't intend—"

"It doesn't matter what they intended," I snapped.

Jonas looked up, "I'm sorry, Sam. Listen, I knew my family was into drugs. They live near Portland and have a deal with…" His voice trailed off and he looked into the distance. "Of course, I knew, but I had no idea your brother worked out this side deal. I would have stopped it. I'm the youngest brother and don't have much power in the family."

I looked over at my brother-in-law. He was holding Katie's hand, and her face looked tortured. She knew what was coming.

I cleared my throat and a hush fell over the pack. "Jonas. By rights, I could have you and your family exiled. You should have known. You should have told me. But I give you grace. Just help me sort this mess out. Your family is rightfully pissed at us."

The worry vanished from my sister's face. Of course, I wasn't going to exile her, and Jonas had nothing to do with it. "I know what it is like to be exiled. I won't even exile Rhett or Lulu. Anyone who helped them is forgiven. Just come forward now."

I was surprised at the amount of men who came forward, each with a sob story about being hard up for cash. I forgave them all and then looked toward the moon. "It's late."

"Today is your wedding day," my mother said, smiling at us both. "Let's put this trouble aside."

I sighed, "Mom, we are making this quick. I've got too much to do."

"Just come at noon. Father Burke will be here, and we'll keep it low-key," she promised.

I looked over my pack and then stood, taking Maggie's hand. She squeezed it firmly. "Thank you all for being honest with me. Let's hope I can figure this out."

Then I nodded to Maggie. "Shift, darling," I whispered. "Do you remember how to do it?"

She nodded and glowed as she shifted, more quickly than the first time. The rest of the pack broke out in applause and I joined her. We touched noses and ran off into the night. The new day was close at hand, and I needed a bit of rest before I jumped into the adventure of the rest of my life with this beautiful woman.

CHAPTER 11
BAIL

woke up later than I intended, glancing over at Maggie, her brown hair spread over the pillow. Already, a glow of health had returned, and she opened her eyes as I bent over to kiss her.

She sat up and stretched, looking like a long lean cat in the sun from the window. "I'm starving. But I feel soooo good today!" she said as I stood in front of my closet, scratching my head.

"What to wear, what to wear," I mused, my fingers running over a few dress shirts and blazers.

Maggie jumped up next to me, her hands falling on the black suit I had worn to Beth and Dan's wedding. "This," she said, pulling out the jacket for me, and then grabbing a white and black-striped tie from a hanger on the back of the door. "And this."

I beamed, "Thank you. And what are *you* wearing to the wedding?"

She shook her finger at me, "You'll see later. Now, I'm hungry."

We both took showers, getting squeaky clean. As I was blow-drying my hair, my phone rang. I winced and picked it up, stepping out of the bathroom.

"Sam. This is Chad Duchamp. I was hoping you could come to the law office today." He sounded brisk and irritable.

"Yeah, I was going to stop by this morning and drop off the retainer and bail money," I said, sweat beginning to break out on my lip. Money that I didn't have… money that I needed to borrow.

"Yeah, just wanted to let you know that the final cost is going to be $8,000 to retain me. What have you decided on for the bail?"

I gulped. My choices were to either put up Silverthorn land as collateral, pay the entire amount myself, or use a bail bondsman, which would still cost cash, just a lot less. "We will use the bondsman."

"Good. That's a solid choice. I'm headed off to court at 10 am. Can you be here by then?"

I glanced at the clock. It was 8:30. "Yeah. If I hurry," I said. Maggie came out of the bathroom wrapped in her robe.

"Don't be late," Chad said and hung up the phone. With a sigh, I looked over at Maggie. "I've got a few errands to run this morning. I'll be back to pick you up in a few hours."

"Good. That gives me time to call Beth. She wanted to come over this morning and help me get ready," Maggie said. "And I'll tell her the good news."

Heading out, I looked over the quiet salon. I wondered if the Clip and Cut would open up right away. We certainly needed the cash. But I wasn't going to push her. She had just recovered from near death, after all. And changing into a werewolf, although she seemed to be handling it well, wasn't for the faint of heart.

Mt. Storm Motors opened at nine, and I pulled in right at the top of the hour. I got out of my shabby truck, smoothing down my tie. A salesman strode up, wearing a black jacket with the four-leaf clover logo on his left breast. I didn't recognize him. *He must not be a townie.*

"Hi! Welcome! I'm Joe. How can I help you today? Are you looking to trade?" He looked over my truck, his lip curling in disdain.

"No, actually. I need to talk to Buster this morning," I said casually, not stopping as I headed to the main office.

"Buster isn't available," he said, trying to stop me. "But I'm sure I can help you. Do you need help with financing? We have some great interest rates available. I have the paperwork right here," he said, leaning over as we passed a wooden desk by the entrance and snagging a clipboard with some papers.

I waved him away. "No, I need to see Buster."

Buster's office was in the back, separated from the main sales area by a large glass wall. I could see him crouched over his desk, going over some ledgers with a pencil and a thick book. He was wearing the same jacket as the salesman, and I noticed a bald spot in the middle of his bright red hair. He was going over the numbers carefully, rubbing his beard as he concentrated.

He glanced up, and through the glass, I could see him smile. A crafty look came into his eyes. He knew why I was here. A leprechaun can always smell desperation.

Buster jumped up from his chair, threw open his door, and held out his arms. "Sam Silverthorn. I was wondering when you were going to give up and grace my doorstep. Come in, come in," he said, his voice jolly and bright.

I glanced back at Joe, the salesman, whose face fell. He didn't have to despair for long because another customer pulled into the lot, and he was out the door before they could even come to a full stop.

Buster was a little person, but his personality made up for his short stature. He had a booming voice, which made you wonder where it came from. "That's my new salesman, Joe. He's an eager beaver, that's for sure. Now, come on into my office and let's talk."

My mouth went dry as I sat down on the most uncomfortable chair I'd ever sat in.

Buster grinned, took his seat across from me, and clasped his hands together. "Tell me, Sam. How much do you need?"

I hesitated. "Buster. I didn't want to do this. You know that. I'm in a spot…"

He nodded, a gleam came into his eyes. "I heard your brothers got arrested yesterday. News travels fast in a small town. I also heard through the grapevine you were getting married today. Congratulations."

"Thank you," I said, notching a finger under my shirt collar. "It's just going to be a small service, but you're welcome to come if you would like. We are having the party on Silverthorn land at noon."

Buster nodded, "Thank you for the invite. I also heard the cops were out poking around yesterday. Your stills get busted? Is that why you need a loan?"

I sighed and rubbed my hand over my face. Then my eyes settled on him. "No, they didn't find anything. I was able to warn my family. But we did lose the current batch, and Junior and Randy got arrested… but for drugs, not shine."

"Drugs?" Buster said, keeping his eyes on me.

"It's a long story. I need to bail them out. I need a bit of cash until we can get the shine running again."

Buster leaned back in his chair, keeping his eyes on me as he popped his knuckles. "I'm a businessman, Sam. I can help you out, but I'm worried you won't be able to pay me back. The gossip line in this town says the Silverthorns are broke as a joke."

"I'm getting too old for these games, Buster. Are you going to give me a loan or not? I need $20,000."

"Well, see, Sam… I don't just give out money to anyone who walks through this door. I didn't build the biggest leprechaun pot of gold in North America by being all charitable."

"I understand. I'm good for the money," I said, desperation rising. "I can repay it in like a year. We can set up monthly payments."

"That's not good enough, Sam. But, listen, I think you're a smart old cookie. I would consider making an investment."

"What kind of investment?" I asked, my warning bells ringing. It was entirely possible Buster might be trying to pull a trick on me.

"I've wondered for years why you didn't take your moonshining legal. Craft liquors are all the rage right now."

"It's a huge investment, Buster. We're talking hundreds of thousands of dollars."

"Yeah, I figured. What if you let me invest in Silverthorn Moonshine? We'll build a factory, get the permits, hire your family and even more locals… it's a win-win for everyone."

"And what do you get out of this deal?" I asked, raising my eyebrows.

"I get the satisfaction of giving back to the local community and improving Mt. Storm," he said, looking at me with a little smile.

"I don't buy it." I shook my head. "There's something else?"

"Free moonshine for life?" he asked with a chuckle. He bent

over, opened his desk drawer, and pulled out an empty mason jar. "I'm empty. Sounds like I can't get any for a bit."

"Sorry," I said with a chuckle. "You'll have to stand in line with everyone else. What do you really want, Buster?"

"You got me. I want a 49% interest in the company. You can pay me back the seed money over time, but in the meantime, everyone will be shoveling in money so fast, it'll make your head spin."

"I need to think about it," I said, clutching the arms of the chair. It was everything I had ever wanted, delivered to me on a silver plate. *Why does it feel so wrong?*

Buster didn't seem to like that answer. He frowned and then reached back into his drawer, pulling out a contract. He scribbled down a few numbers in blank spaces and then pushed it across the table, throwing a pen on top. "It's a standard contract I use. Sign it now or you get nothing."

I felt rising panic. I picked up the thick stack of paper and read it over. It was a pretty basic contract. My mouth went dry when I read the loan amount—20 million dollars. Several more zeroes than what I walked in here today looking for.

Silence fell around us as I flipped through the pages, looking for any leprechaun trick that stood out. I caught a clause at the bottom: "Loan can be called at any time," I read out loud.

"It's just lawyer mumbo jumbo," Buster said, waving my concerns away. "Sign now or this generous deal disappears. Hey, I'll even throw a new truck into the deal." He looked out the glass of his office, across the floor, and out the window to my sad truck sitting at the curb.

This was everything I wanted. It would solve all of our problems and give us a chance to take Silverthorn Moonshine national. Biting my lip, I picked up the pen and signed my name, hoping I wasn't making a huge mistake.

"Looks like you're my new best friend, Sam. You and I are going to work real close in the next year, building the business from the ground up. Let me show you something," he said, standing up.

I stood, expecting him to exit the office. Instead, he lowered the blinds and then locked the door.

I looked around his office, wondering what he needed privacy for. With a grin, he stepped over to a wall of file cabinets. Above it hung a calendar of the Irish countryside with a rainbow stretching across the photo. Imagine my surprise when he reached back behind the cabinet on the end and pulled a latch. The cabinet swung outward, revealing a staircase that led down into a brightly lit room.

"Come, come. Let me show you something most people don't get a chance to see. My leprechaun trove." He gestured to me with a smile, then tapped his head. Instantly, his black jacket was replaced with what can only be described as a leprechaun outfit.

My mouth dropped as I looked at his black shiny shoes with buckles, his green overalls, ending right at the knee, and his black top hat. To complete the get-up, he carried a twisted cane that looked like the root of some type of tree. "I've got to play the part, you know," he giggled, leading me down the stairs.

I felt like I was in some kind of twilight zone, and my old knees twinged as I took the stairs. This was a basement, obviously, with bright sterile lights and a tile floor. We stood now in front of vault doors—stainless steel and opposing.

"This is a high-security vault. We've got lasers, video surveillance, and to anyone unlucky enough to try to steal my horde, automatic machine guns."

My eyes went wide as he reached the door, glanced at me suspiciously, and then covered his hand as he typed in a pin code. I heard the numbers beeping, and then a happy chirp sounded before the door swung open.

"My riches, accumulated over the last 100 years. When I arrived in Mt. Storm, I was a wee lad with the starter horde, gifted to me by my father. I've grown it to one of the largest in North America," he said proudly, puffing out his chest.

He was obviously a man proud of his accomplishments. I stepped past him, into the vault.

It was huge… like a massive underground warehouse. There must have been forty rows of shelves, covered with every type of bill, coin, jewel, and metal bar you could imagine. One entire wall contained what appeared to be priceless art masterpieces. I blinked—it was overwhelming. "Why don't you use a bank?" I asked, feeling a hot flash coming on.

"It's *my* pot o' gold," Buster shrugged. "Us leprechauns don't really believe in banks. The bigger horde we build, the more powerful we are in leprechaun society."

"So, you must be really powerful," I said, giving him a side glance. He was stroking a bar of gold absently like it was a cat.

"Very powerful. But, really, only in North America. There are some European leprechauns who make me look like a small potato."

"Really?" I said, walking down an aisle. The smell of money hung in the air. I reached out to touch a bag of coins.

"No, no, no. No touching," Buster said sharply, and I pulled my hand back like it had been burned.

"Sorry," I mumbled. He stood, cross-armed, looking at me sternly.

"This is what we want," he said, going over to a shelf with only a handful of strange coins scattered across the grey metal surface. He picked one up, held it between his forefinger and thumb, and examined it. Then, with a nod, he passed it to me.

It was heavy and felt like solid gold. The front was a fearsome-looking troll-like creature. Its hands were raised, and between the teeth and the claws, I didn't want to meet this creature in a dark alley. I flipped it over and saw a resemblance of Buster carved in the back. As I handled it, it caused my palm to tingle. "What is this?" I asked, feeling it warm from my body heat.

"It's a special coin that can be used just like money. You show it to the vendor, and everything will be taken care of. Don't lose it," he warned. "It's worth its weight in gold and more. I'll have to hunt it down if you do."

I nodded and slipped it into my pocket. "Thanks," I said, taking a last look at the place. I thought the whole situation was wild, if I was being honest.

"Now, what color truck do you want?" Buster asked with a grin.

CHAPTER 12
DUCHAMP AND SONS

I pulled up at the curb, not really believing I just drove off Buster's lot with a brand new shiny white Ford 250. It was smooth, didn't sound like a dump truck, and the AC worked.

Literally, Buster grabbed the keyring off a large board, handed it to me with a wink, and then walked out to the lot. No papers to sign—nada.

His salesman did give me the stink eye, probably mad he had lost out on a commission. I drove off the lot and spied them moving my trade-in to the back. Farewell, old truck. You served me well. But then I drove through town with one last errand to run before the wedding.

Parking in front of the building, I looked at the window, painted in gold. The lettering read: "Duchamp and Sons." As far as I knew, Chad only had two small children. Certainly neither of them were old enough to partner with him.

I went into the office and spied his secretary, typing away at a keyboard.

Glancing up at the clock, I saw that it was nearly 10 am. I had talked to my mom on the way over here and assured her I was working on getting my brothers out of the clink, and still would be there by noon for the nuptials.

"Can I help you?" she asked briskly. She seemed a little harried as she tucked a pencil into her brown hair. She wore no makeup, and a plain blouse and brown slacks with a hideous green sweater over it all. Her name plate read Terri Quinn.

"Hi, Terri!" I said, smiling with more enthusiasm than I felt. "I have an appointment with Chad Duchamp!"

Terri glanced at me sternly and then checked her schedule. She nodded and picked up her phone, "Your appointment is here."

I waited a moment, and Chad bounced out of a closed door. His face was red and he was sweating heavily. His blond hair was thinning on top, and he had a pot belly. He wore a white shirt and a tie already loosened around his neck.

"Sam Silverthorn," he said, his voice full of fake enthusiasm as he offered me his hand and then shook it heartily. "Come in."

I went into the office, taking a seat on a highly polished leather and wood sofa. He eased down into his chair with a grunt. The desk was covered with papers, the computer screen off.

I spied a mason jar, certainly Silverthorn shine, tucked behind a picture of his family. His wife, Lucy, and their two little kids, captured in the flash of a camera. The oldest looked to be about one. Lucy was holding a newborn baby boy in the picture. She was smiling at the camera, but her eyes looked tired.

Beth proudly told me she had a new little grandson, but I had not met him. "You have a beautiful family," I noted, nodding toward the picture.

"Yeah, kids are a lot and Lucy is a bitch when she's pregnant.

Two and done." He chuckled and I felt repulsion at his statement.

I cleared my throat and said, "About your payment…"

"You brought it all?" Chad said, his eyes looking over me greedily.

I nodded and pulled out the coin, holding it up for him to see.

"Dang. Is that what I think it is?" Chad asked, holding out his hand.

I nodded, handing it over. He inspected it, his face unreadable. With a sigh, he handed it back. "Consider your bill paid then. You've made a deal with Buster, huh?"

"I didn't have much choice, did I?" I said sarcastically.

"Well, Buster's coin is as good as gold. Interesting really, the payment will just show up as a check sometime next week. I don't know how he knows. Magic, I guess," Chad said, leaning back in his chair and clasping his hands behind his head. His eyes never left me.

I didn't offer any other comment. There was nothing more to say.

Finally, Chad broke the silence and leaned forward. "Guess I'll head to the courthouse. Your brothers have some serious drug charges, but as this is their first offense, the judge should go light on them."

"Good," I said. "Any chance you can get them out before noon?"

"Noon? I'm a lawyer, not a miracle worker." Chad gave a little chuckle and started to shuffle through his paperwork. Finding what he needed, he held up the papers. "I'm going to walk over to the courthouse and get this party started. Are you coming with me?"

"I've got a wedding to make," I said with a smile, adjusting my necktie.

"Of course," he said. "Marriage, the old ball and chain. You're a little old to be getting hitched."

I shook my head, "I'm fifty. Haven't you heard? Fifty is the new twenty."

He laughed, "I wish. Sometimes I dream about faking my own death and taking off. Two bad I got tied down with kids."

He was so gross, I couldn't stand him. I felt bad for Beth's daughter. *What a prick.*

Standing up, I shook his hand. "Let me know if things go wrong."

"You've got that magic coin. I'll be happy to take Buster's money. We will fight hard," Chad said, grabbing his blazer off the back of his chair and struggling to put it on. He tightened his tie and shouted out to his secretary, "Terri. I'm off to the courthouse. Call me if anything promising pops up."

"Yes, boss," she said briskly, looking at him over her reading glasses. I got the impression she hated him, but a job was a job.

CHAPTER 13
WEDDING

Katie was waiting for me when I pulled up. She was wearing a light blue summer dress with a white rose tucked behind her ear. "Hey, I'm glad you decided to show up. We were getting worried," she said, and then looked down at the truck. "Is this new?"

"It is," I said, not explaining as I glanced at the shiny new dash clock. There was plenty of time. "I was busy bailing the boys out and trying to stay out of financial ruin."

Katie laughed "I'm not sure buying a new truck is the way to do that, but your old truck was a bit crusty."

I shrugged and got out of the truck, buttoning my jacket, and giving her a grin. She grabbed my arm, "Maggie's in there, no seeing the bride before the ceremony. Mom told me I'm supposed to take care of you."

"Okay," I laughed. "Where do you want me?"

I shook hands and greeted the pack, then stood waiting, looking anxiously toward the house where Maggie had been ensconced getting ready. In front of me was the stone circle, a small fire lit, mostly for the ceremony.

Father Burke stood in front of me, in his full priest robes, with his hands clasped. His gray hair shone in the light. He smiled and threw his hands up dramatically. "It's a lovely day for a wedding."

Beth Potentia came out of the house, beaming widely. She was the maid of honor as her and Maggie had been friends since they were kids.

Her team even joined her this morning. Easton, his massive form looking ridiculous on the small bench sitting next to his lovely wife, Tina. Beau and Dallas Drake were behind them, their eyes scanning the gathering group. Even Garret, perching on Easton's shoulder in his raven form, his beady black eyes staring at me.

Indeed, it was a lovely day for a wedding, and my mother had outdone herself. Bundles of wildflowers were tucked between benches, festooned with white ribbon. On a table was a roasted pig, potato salads, and pots of beans waiting for us to all dig in. Mason jars, repurposed to hold small candles, were tucked around the clearing.

Out of the corner of my eye, I was shocked to see Junior and Randy run up in their wolf forms, freshly released from jail. A mutter ran through the crowd, but they didn't even look at me before going into Mom's house, probably to clean up after their night in the county jail.

They slipped out a few minutes later in dress clothes. Junior was glaring at me, and Randy wouldn't meet my eye. I guess they weren't thankful I had taken the time on my wedding day to bail them out.

Finally, Dennis hit enter on a laptop, and H.O.L.Y by Florida Georgia line started to play. I chuckled, Maggie for sure picked out the playlist for today. She knew I loved sappy country love songs—a leftover from my long-haul trucking days.

Before the bride even appeared, I started to get choked up. Katie came and stood by my side, and bent over and kissed my cheek, "Happy wedding day, sister." I blinked back tears, and then Maggie finally appeared.

It was everything I could do to not break into a sob. My beloved stood, smiling at me, a bouquet of wildflowers in her hand. A vision of health. Somewhere, she had found a wedding dress. It was long, and lacey, and her hair tumbled over her shoulders.

Maggie walked across the grass to me, and Junior, on the front bench, scowled. He caught me glaring at him. Randy elbowed him sharply, and Junior sat up straight and fixed his face, although his eyes betrayed his true feelings.

Father Burke turned to the crowd. "Good day, fine folks. We are gathered here today to unite Sam and Maggie. I've had the joy to know both of them, and I've got to say, it's about time!"

There was a chuckle throughout the crowd. I took Maggie's hands and stared into her eyes. "I love you," I mouthed to her, and her eyes crinkled with delight.

"Now, I would appreciate it if none of you here today told my boss, the one in the Vatican, that I performed this ceremony. We have a fundamental disagreement, but I know love is love. They can kick me out if they want, but I don't think they'll do that."

As Father Burke performed the wedding ceremony, my eyes focused on Maggie. The day was warm, and I felt sweat trickle down my back. I couldn't wait to get this suit coat off. Finally, it was bride-kissing time. Our lips touched and the pack cheered.

My mom sure knew how to put on a fine hootenanny. The fiddles, banjos, and mandolins were pulled out, and the toe-tapping music began.

Mom had pulled out the last of the moonshine—I recognized it from the cellar. The mason jars were dusty and I realized this was my dad's private stash. Some of his experimental berry blends, and a couple aged in barrels.

With the moonshine flowing and music playing, the fun began. But I only had eyes for Maggie.

"I'm so happy you're my wife," I bent over and whispered in her ear.

"Do you think they all like me?" she asked, biting her lip.

"They love you," I assured her, giving both her hands a squeeze.

Beth Potentia found us. Garret, in his raven form, was sitting on her shoulder, looking majestic. His beady black eyes stared at us, and then he took off, flying high up into the sky. I guess he wasn't one for partying. Beth reached over and gave us both a hug. "A beautiful wedding. I'm so happy you invited me. Maggie told me about her change. I know the pack can be a little skittish about outsiders. How's it going?"

"It's a bit new. But it seems to be going well." I looked over at my brothers, who were huddled together at the far end of the clearing, seemingly in serious talks. Something was going on and I needed to figure it out.

"I feel good, Beth," Maggie said with a smile. "My strength has returned. I'm looking forward to starting the salon back up but it's so daunting. I'll have to hire some people, contact old customers. I feel like the passion for that has left me. Life is so fleeting, you know."

"It is. I've seen heaven and hell, and being happy in this life is the key to being happy in the afterlife. Miserable people don't end up in good places." Beth sighed and looked pensive for a moment.

I looked over at Easton, with a small glass of moonshine wrapped in his huge ham fist, dancing with my brothers. A chuckle escaped my lips and I saw Beau and Dallas Drake testing out the different flavors of moonshine with Junior and Randy over by the picnic table. "You are practically family, Beth. But thanks for not bringing Dan."

Her face turned serious. "I wanted to let you know that it could have been a lot worse. Dan heard the feds were on your brother's tail and put himself in a place to try to protect you. I was worried you would get arrested but thank God you didn't."

I took a swig of my untouched moonshine, blueberry flavor, and grimaced at her words. "I know. Thank him for me, would you? I'll deal with my brothers later."

"Sam! Come and dance with me!" Maggie said, her eyes bright as she held out her hands. Take Me to Church by Hozier came on, and I couldn't resist. A little bleak for a wedding, but if you didn't listen too closely to the words, it was perfect.

CHAPTER 14
CROSSROADS

took a few days after the wedding to relax with my new bride. Maggie was full of life and vitality. We celebrated our nuptials by getting rid of the hospital bed in the downstairs office and moving back upstairs to our apartment.

"Meat. I need meat," Maggie said, taking a raw steak out of a foam store package and holding it in both hands. She took a bite and nodded her head in approval as the juices ran down her chin.

I chuckled and handed her a paper towel. "It's the new werewolf thing. You'll crave raw meat for a while."

She took another big bite, chewing thoroughly. I leaned my elbows on our kitchen table, my laptop and cell phone at my side. All morning, I had been making phone calls about the new moonshine business. Later tonight, we had a pack meeting scheduled, where I would let my kin know what I'd been up to.

"I've been thinking, Sam," she said, putting the raw meat down on the blood-soaked meat tray and licking her fingers.

"Yes?" I asked as I reached across the table and took her hand, staring deeply into her eyes.

"I'm considering renting out the downstairs," she said with a small smile on her face.

"What? You mean close down Maggie's Clip and Cut?" I asked, disbelief lacing my voice.

"Yes. I've lost the passion for it. I've spent half my life working here, tied to this one place. I think it's time for a change. I never really liked cutting hair, it's sort of something I just fell into."

"But where are the nursing home ladies going to go to get their hair set?" I teased, my eyes twinkling.

"You know, Mary opened up a little shop in her basement in the holler after I got sick. All my old customers go to her now. It's going to be tough to get this place started back up again."

I looked out the open window of our apartment. A cool breeze fluttered the sheer curtain, and the smell of sunshine and asphalt filled the room. It was a warm rush hour in Mt. Storm, and the street parking was almost full.

When we opened a tasting room, Maggie and I wouldn't have time to run this shop. "I like that idea. It's a great location, and the downstairs, with its tin ceiling and wood floors, could easily be converted into a gift shop or café. And of course, I would love you to help out with the tasting room. I'm going to have my hands full, that's for sure."

"You'll let me help decorate the new tasting room?" I could already tell she was dreaming up floor plans.

"Of course." I smiled. "How does Silverthorn's Whiskey Room sound?"

"Perfect," she said, picking up the meat and taking another big bite.

Just then, a raven flew through the window, startling us. It landed and began to change.

I watched the purple glow carefully as it grew and

transformed into Garret. He stood with his arms crossed. "Sorry to interrupt you, but I need Sam right away. Jesus sent me to tell you your brothers are up to no good."

I stood quickly, nearly toppling over my chair. My face was white and anxiety hammered in my chest. They had refused to answer my calls since the wedding, and I'd intended to hunt them down today. "What's going on?"

"They are headed on foot out of town," Garret said, glancing back over his shoulder.

"Dang it!" I turned to Maggie. "They aren't supposed to leave Mt. Storm. If Dan finds out, or they get spotted, they could end up back in jail. I've got to hunt them down."

"Go," she said urgently, putting her meat back down. "Do you need my help?"

I hesitated for a moment, then shook my head. "No, I need to talk to them myself."

"Be careful, my love," Maggie said, getting up and putting the rest of the raw steak into the fridge.

I nodded, then turned to Garret. "Lead the way." I hurried down the stairs, opening the back door as I began to shift. By the time I reached the back alley, I was in full wolf form. Glancing up at Garret flying overhead I watched him turn to the north. I kept running, keeping him in sight as I ran full-out through town.

People barely blinked as I raced by. As soon as I was able, I exited town, slipping into the trees. We were headed due north, seemingly toward the state park.

Overhead, a few more ravens appeared, and I realized that the rest of the coven had joined. I moved as quietly as possible down game paths, twice startling deer taking cover from the heat of the day.

Stopping in a clearing just at the edge of the state park, I looked up. A bird circled down and then the form of Jesus Armando appeared in the shadow of a pine. The sharp smell of pine resin hung in the air as I shifted into my human form and approached. The shade felt good on my sweaty skin, and I tried to catch my breath from the long run. I flopped down and leaned against the pine tree, feeling the rough bark under my black t-shirt.

Jesus stretched his arms, swinging them from side to side. I supposed flying was just as exhausting as running. "Your brothers are in the park. It looks like they might be waiting for someone." Jesus said, "We've been keeping an eye on them, afraid they might start dealing again. The holler has been peaceful and quiet since they got busted. We would like to keep it that way."

"Thank you, Jesus. I'm sorry my brothers are causing so much trouble. I want to find out what's going on. Can you lead me to where they are? I'll try to stay hidden," I said.

Jesus looked up into the sky, shading his eyes with his hand. Then he pointed. "See, Carlos is perched at the top of that tree. Garret and Paul are flying up overhead."

I saw the raven in the distance at the very top of a scraggly-looking Virginia Pine. Nodding, I said, "Let's go. I'll stay out of sight."

———

I put one paw down carefully on a tuft of dry grass, feeling it break under my weight. Creeping forward through the tall grass, I approached the path.

It was a crossroads of sorts. A place where two trails met. A rough sign, letters burned into the weathered wood, pointed to the north. It read: "Indian Cave 1.2 miles." The other piece of the sign pointed south, and it read: "Parking Lot 2.2 miles."

Junior leaned up against the bark of a tree, examining his fingernails. He took a small knife out of his pocket and worked it under the nail, cleaning out dirt.

Randy sat on a nearby log in the shade, his back to me. He was checking his cell phone. I lowered my body to the ground, feeling the warmth of the earth, and inched forward, anxious to hear their discussion. Why were they alone out here at the state park? They must be up to no good, there was no other explanation.

I sat perfectly still, keeping my head low and my ears forward. A bee buzzed around my head, but I tuned it out. Finally, Junior folded his knife back up and put it in his pocket.

"Hopefully, she's here soon. All this waiting sucks," Junior said.

"I don't know, Junior. This makes me nervous. What if…"

"We don't have any other choice. We've tried to take over the pack by undermining Sam, but she's just too well-liked. I thought for certain if we delayed the batches of moonshine and everyone had to tighten their belts, they would turn against her. But everyone loves her," Junior said, his voice dripping with sarcasm.

"She promised she would help us," Randy said, his voice sounding hopeful. "If Sam happens to meet with a tragic accident, the vote will be up again. You're the only logical choice."

"I am, aren't I?" Junior said, and I could see a smug look on his face from across the clearing. I longed to jump out of the bushes and smack it off his insolent little face, but I really wanted to see who he was meeting here.

I didn't have to wait long because, after a few minutes of idle chit-chat from the boys about how much of a pain in the ass I was, a shadow appeared on the north trail, coming from the direction of the caves.

I caught a whiff of brimstone and felt a whine rising in my throat, which I caught in the nick of time. Lowering my head to the ground, I wanted to make myself as invisible as possible. Overhead, I saw the ravens in the trees. One lifted into the air, and turned toward Mt. Storm, but I couldn't tell which one it was.

She stepped out into the sunlight, and I instantly recognized Sarah Morris. Well, I recognized her features at least. She had certainly changed. From her long blond hair, two horns emerged, curling down past her ears. Her blue eyes had widened and deepened in color. Her nails were now claw-like— six inches long and razor-sharp. Her claws were painted red, and I wondered if there were manicurists in hell.

Sarah wore a strange outfit, more fit for a heavy metal concert than a leisurely stroll in the state park. A jean jacket with the sleeves cut off displayed her now sculpted biceps and forearms. A megadeath t-shirt underneath, and a pair of jean shorts cut so short, her bottom hung out the back.

She had what we girls liked to call, "junk in the trunk." A muscular bottom that the Kardashians would be jealous of.

Sarah Morris was a named demon now. Years ago, Dan Comstock had shot her dead. Unfortunately, she went straight to hell and gained powers she didn't have before. If he'd just kept his service piece in his pocket, she wouldn't be such a problem.

"Hello, boys. Thank you for answering my call," Sarah said, throwing her long hair over one shoulder daintily with her long red claws.

"I sure was surprised when your boss turned up in my vanity mirror," Junior said with a chuckle.

Sarah smirked at him, "Yes, it's a good way to communicate. He can't come through as easily as me. The minute a gate opens, Beth and her gang of idiots turn up and try to ruin our fun. I managed to give her the slip last time though. So, with me on this side, and Lucifer on the other, we make the perfect team." She stepped forward, looking at him intently. Junior was nervous and shifted on his feet, wiping his forehead with one hand.

"So, you want us to do something? He mentioned that he would get rid of Sam for us if I could just help him out," Randy said, his voice hopeful.

I was getting angry at my traitorous brothers. They were plotting in the worst way possible.

"I need you to do just a little favor for me," she said, one hand on her hip. She swayed closer to him, her eyes fixed on him seductively.

"Uhhh, what do you need? That's why we are here," Junior said, and I could smell his sweat and fear. It stank, and my nose curled.

She put her arms around his neck and then arched her back. Her claws trailed over his shoulders, and I saw a muscle twitch in his face. "I need you to take Eliana Potentia and bring her to the Indian Cave."

"Take her?" Randy said, a note of disbelief in his voice, "She's just a little girl. I don't know if I'm up for kidnapping,"

Sarah's head snapped to him and a dangerous look crossed her face. In an instant, she was near him, her claws outstretched. "You know, I need a sacrifice to open the portal. You'll do."

Randy raised his hands in panic. "No! I was just stating my reservations. We can work together, no problem."

"Very good," Sarah said, stepping back. Then she paused,

and at that instant, the wind changed. Her nose moved, sniffing. Then her eyes met mine through the waving grass.

Caught! I thought to myself, rising up from the tall grass. My tail flicked. She certainly smelled me, and now I was in deep trouble.

"Well, well, well. Sam has decided to pay us a little visit," Sarah said, waving a hand. Behind me, fire erupted in the dry grass, cutting off my only escape.

Seeing that there was no way out but forward, I snarled and lunged at her, my jaw outstretched. I latched onto her arm as my body crashed into her.

I know I shouldn't have taken on a named demon by myself. It was pure stupidity on my part, but I didn't have many options. With the fire blazing behind me, and my escape path blocked off, I did what was a natural instinct—I attacked.

What I didn't count on was her pure strength. Unlike a normal human, she was as sturdy as a tree. When my body hit her, she didn't even stumble. And as my teeth bit at her, it didn't even break her skin. She laughed and held her arm out. My body hung limply with my entire weight dangling in the wind.

"No! Don't hurt her!" Randy yelled. That was the last thing I heard before Sarah's fist closed and smashed me in the head. My jaw released involuntarily, and I crumbled to the dirt and started to shift into my human form. This wasn't good. I was injured badly. No werewolf automatically shifted unless they were in a very bad way. I felt blood dripping down my face and reached up with a shaking hand to touch it. My head hurt like the worst migraine I'd ever experienced. The world faded out to a tiny black dot. Well, three of them actually. My vampire friends, flying straight and true to Mt. Storm.

CHAPTER 15
JUNIOR SILVERTHORN

, Junior Silverthorn, didn't expect Sarah to knock out my sister so easily. Maybe it was a sign that our leader was weak. For sure, I wouldn't have let the named one get to me so easily.

The clearing was quiet, and Randy and I just looked at each other. Fear was palpable between us. We were in deep now. No way to turn back. What we had done would earn us an immediate exile from the pack… unless we could turn the story around and make ourselves look like the victims here.

But that thought didn't change the fact that my sister, Sam, was crumpled in front of us, bleeding from her nose and ears. Sarah's eyes turned to me and I felt icy fear run down my spine.

Three ravens swirled into the air, and Randy's eyes flicked to them. "Junior, those are vampires! Shit, why didn't I notice them before? It's Jesus and his gang, and Garret hangs out with them. They'll tell Beth."

In fact, I could hear the distant sound of police sirens. "They are already on the way," Sarah said, and bent down, easily picking up the limp body of my sister, holding her under one arm like an inconvenient package. "I'm going back to the gate. Get the girl."

"Let's go, brother," Randy said, changing into his wolf form. He was silver with a black snout. I nodded and switched at the same time. Both of us took off through the woods, swinging wide of the parking lot to avoid both the police and Potentia Security.

We tried to stay out of sight, running through the woods. Once, I caught sight of a raven overhead, but I bolted back into the deep underbrush, with Randy hot on my heels.

Together, we made it to the edge of town where I had parked the cargo van. Before stepping out in the open, we changed into our human forms, walking briskly to the van and opening the driver's side door. Randy was breathing heavily. "We nearly got caught."

In my pocket, my cell phone rang—it was Beth. I picked up the phone, holding a finger to my lips.

"Junior! What have you done with Sam? Where is she? Garret told me you met with Sarah."

"Stay out of Silverthorn business, Beth. This is none of your concern," I said, rubbing a hand over my face, hiding a nasty smile.

"Where is she?" Beth screamed at me through the phone line, her voice full of urgency.

Without a word, I ended the call and then sat, my thoughts whirling. "It's 2 o'clock. School's almost out. Let's see what we can do." I threw my cell phone into the console and clicked my seatbelt closed.

I started the van and drove toward Mt. Storm. Once I reached Main Street, I headed directly to the school. The parking lot was starting to fill, with parents waiting to pick up their kids as soon as the bell rang. I parked illegally in the fire lane and turned to Randy. "You take the driver's seat. Don't let anyone tow us. I'll be back soon."

As I approached the school, my wheels were turning. Maybe I should have planned this out a little better, but I felt confident. I had gone here, long ago, and I knew the school secretary well, having bribed her with flowers and gifts throughout the years. With our wild pack pups, it helped to have the school secretary on your side.

I strode in with a concerned look on my face. The school secretary looked up, a pen held in her hand. Myra Bunn was a middle-aged sweetheart who went to Mt. Storm Lutheran Church like everyone else in this little town. "Junior! So nice to see you today! How's the family? I do miss those little vixens."

I laughed and leaned against the counter casually, feeling the cold laminate under my fingers. "Seems like only yesterday I was a student here. I sure did get in my share of trouble."

"Kids grow up so fast," She put down her pen and leaned forward. "One minute, you're getting calls from the school, and then next thing you know, they are flying away to college. My youngest just started at West Virginia Tech," Myra said, a wistful look on her face.

"That's fantastic. Good to hear. I'm actually here on business. You know, we work with Potentia Security. Beth just got called out and she's worried about Eliana. She asked that I swing by and pick her up."

Myra paused, a concerned look on her face. "Well, you know, I can't just let you take her. You aren't on the list."

"I know, it's a tough situation. Look, Beth called me and asked that I pick her up. See?" I held up the phone, showing Beth Potentia was my last call.

"Maybe I should call her mom?" Myra said. Just then, the school bell rang and kids started to flood out.

It wasn't a large school, just two long halls. All the students filed out to the buses, which were lined up at the front.

"You know what? Don't worry about it," I said with a shrug. This wasn't working, and I had to switch gears fast. "She can get on the bus and I can meet her at the house. I'm supposed to watch her until Beth or Dan gets home."

Myra's hand wavered near the phone, uncertain. I smiled and waved goodbye, opening up the office door and striding out confidently. The halls were filled with kids, all flowing out of the building. I caught sight of a few of my kin, Silverthorn pack youth. They all shouted and ran over to give me a hug. I wasted valuable minutes untangling myself before the kids all tumbled for the big #4 bus, headed for home.

Thankfully, I quickly caught sight of Eliana, walking with a little blond girl. They were chatting animatedly, their little heads inches from each other.

"Eliana!" I shouted to get her attention. She looked up at me, her dark eyes not recognizing me at first. To be honest, I hadn't thought this part out. She'd only met me a handful of times, mostly when I had business up at the big house.

Eliana Potentia stopped in her tracks. "Who are you?" she asked, gripping her books tighter to her chest.

"I'm Junior Silverthorn. We've met at your grandfather's house. You might know my sister, Sam."

"I know Sam!" Her face brightened. "She's Maggie's wife! Mom just went to the wedding and I made her a card!"

"That's right. Your mom called me. She needs me to pick you up. Your mom and Sam are on a mission," I said, taking a step forward and holding out my hand.

Eliana seemed hesitant. She looked over at her little friend. "Violet and I have a playdate today. I'm supposed to go home and check in with Zara."

I had no idea who Zara was, but I wouldn't let the threat of some babysitter stand in my way. "There has been a change of plans."

"Eliana. Dad said we aren't supposed to go with anyone we don't know. Why would your mom send this guy to pick you up? Zara is waiting for you. Zara could pick you up," the little blond girl said, her voice trembling.

Eliana looked at him, her eyes wide. She took a step back. "Yeah, she could. She's picked me up from school before."

"I don't have time for this," I said grumpily. Apparently, I was very bad at trying to be sneaky. My entire plan had gone to pot. It looked like I was going to have to snatch this child the old-fashioned way. I sighed, realizing I was in too deep to turn around now. I lunged forward, grabbing Eliana by her waist.

She screamed right before I managed to clamp a hand over her mouth. She kicked me in the thigh with her pink tennis shoes. *Ouch. That hurt.* She twisted, and it was all I could do to hang on.

"Help! Help! A bad man has Eliana!" Violet shrieked and ran up and kicked me in the other shin. That hurt even worse. The little girl was wearing hard leather cowboy boots.

Now, things were slowing down as my actions caught the attention of teachers helping kids on the bus.

Cursing, I threw Eliana over my shoulder, all while she was clawing and beating at me. Holding her legs tightly as I ran to the van, where I could see Randy sitting at the wheel.

"Stop!" a shrill voice called from my left. I turned slightly and noticed Lucy Duchamp standing at a side entrance, a wand held loosely in her hand. *Dang it!* I forgot Beth's oldest daughter was a teacher here.

"Lucy! Help me!" Eliana shouted. I ran faster, feeling my shirt becoming soaked with my sweat.

And that's when Lucy Duchamp began throwing fireballs at me. I was away from the crowd of kids, and the first fireball hit a few inches from my left foot. I yelped and jumped to the right, where another fireball zipped past my ear.

"Lucy!" Eliana yelled again, tears streaming down her face.

I reached the van. Now, a few parents had joined the chase and I feared they would tear me apart if they managed to get their hands on me. Randy leaned over and opened the passenger side door. I shoved Eliana into the vehicle, jumping in beside her as a fireball hit me on the seat of my pants. Yelping, I slammed the door shut.

It was a mad shuffle as I swatted at my denim jeans to put the flames out. Eliana was sitting in the middle, a murderous look on her face. She lifted her hand and her lips curled.

"Oh, NO! NO!" I shouted, grabbing the kid's hand. She lunged forward, headbutting me. She cracked me hard, and my eyes swam with tears, but I managed to keep a hold of her. A wave of fire hit the van, and I could feel the heat radiating from the glass. "She's trying to burn us alive!"

Sirens wailed behind them. "Cops are here!" Randy said, throwing the van into drive.

"Well, go! GO!" I shouted, the kid held firmly in my arms. "Take the backroads."

We screeched out of the parking lot. Randy barely avoided hitting several minivans. This delivery van wasn't meant for high-speed chases, but with the chaos at the school, we quickly lost the cops in the traffic.

Randy practically put the van on two wheels as he turned down a country road, kicking up gravel and dust into the air. Holding Eliana tight against my chest took everything I had in me. She struggled at first, but then stopped, staring out the window.

"Where are you taking me?" she asked in a scared voice.

"Your dad wants to see you," I said. "And I'm all for parental rights."

She said nothing to that, but I felt wet tears falling on my arm.

"What, you don't want to see your real dad?" I said, looking out the window. Randy was driving way too fast for these country roads, and I didn't have my seat belt on.

"Dan is my real dad. I don't care who my bio dad is. He's scary," Eliana said quietly.

"Well, you're going to meet him. A daughter/father reunion. Isn't it exciting?" I said, trying to put joviality into my voice. If I was being honest, I felt slightly guilty for kidnapping a little girl in broad daylight. I guess I had just got myself in even more trouble than a few drug and moonshining charges.

Kidnapping was most certainly a bail violation. I might have to go into hiding with one of the Kentucky packs. I'm sure they would have me. I could stay with them for a little while, and then sneak back and take control of the pack.

"No. Just let me go. Pull over here. I can find my way home," Eliana pleaded and her voice tore at my heartstrings. I realized that if someone took my kid, I would hunt them down to the ends of the earth. The thought made me uncomfortable, and I caught Randy's eye. He also looked extremely guilty.

"I'm not letting a little girl walk home alone from the middle of the country," I said firmly, looking down at her.

"But you'll kidnap me? Got it," Eliana said, looking at me like I was pure trash.

Another wave of guilt hit me. "Listen, you don't understand. I've been under a lot of pressure, okay? This is the only way to take control of my pack." I tried to reason with her, but she wasn't listening. She was staring out the window. I realized she was looking out the side mirror. A smile came on to her lips.

"What? What's going on?" I said, looking fearfully out the back window of the van. I didn't see anything.

She didn't answer, and Randy took another sharp turn, this time, on a dirt-rutted service road.

"This is the back road into the state park," Randy said, keeping his eyes on the road, both hands gripping the wheel with white knuckles. We hit a rut, going way too fast, and I slammed into the door.

Eliana looked over at Randy and a faraway look came over her face as her eyes glazed over. Then she began to sing:

Ring around the rosie
A pocketful of posies
Ashes, ashes
We all fall down.

"Damn, that's creepy," Randy said, shaking his head. We reached a dirt parking lot with a trailhead. No vehicles were parked here as this was a remote and rarely used entrance. Randy pulled into the lot and threw the van into park. "Luckily, the Indian Cave isn't far from this entrance."

"Let's go before someone tracks us here," I said, eyeing the trailhead. Randy jumped out and went around the side of the car, opening the driver's door for me.

"I'll take her," Randy said, grabbing Eliana firmly by both wrists.

She repeated the nursery rhyme, her body limp. Randy easily threw her over one shoulder, and she hung like a corpse.

I climbed out, looking right and left and licking my lips. The feeling of being watched was strong. That's when I saw the raven landing in the field. "We've got a visitor. Take her, I'll hold this one off."

"Are you sure you can take a vampire? She seems pretty out of it. I could probably just put her back in the van," Randy said, a concerned look on his face.

"No, go. I'll be right behind you," I said, pointing down the path. The vampire was shifting. A purple glow surrounded him, and he grew and twisted into his real form.

It was Carlos—one of Jesus's sidekicks. Randy hurried down the path, and I turned to face him. "If you don't mind, I need to change," I said with a little grin on my face, shifting into my werewolf form. As my body shrunk, I could feel power coming into my limbs. My silver fur gleamed in the bright light. Supernatural power vs supernatural power, and I had the upper hand as vampires were weaker in the daylight.

Carlos's dark eyes stared at me with malice, and he put both his hands up in fists. "You dirty dog. Perro sucio."

I felt anger building, then I snarled and leaped, a growl tearing from my throat. I could smell the vampire, and it was driving me berserk. Vampires were a werewolf's mortal enemy, and for years, I had been forced to work with one—Garret, Beth's little friend. I can't tell you how many times I wanted to crush that little twerp's head in my jaw. This wasn't Garret, but it would do.

Carlos punched me square in the chest, and I went flying back, the breath knocked out of me. I took a moment, letting my breathing slow. Carlos made no move to attack me while I was down. Finally, I recovered and growled as I circled slowly, looking for a break in the vampire's defenses.

"You want more of this? We are evenly matched. There can be no winner here," Carlos said, "Stand down and let me pass."

But I couldn't let him pass. I growled again, lunging at his neck. If I could just get a firm grip, I could shake and snap the vampire's head off its body like dry kindling. But this vampire was smart and lowered his chin, lifting a leg and kicking me in the ribs.

I whimpered and scampered back from the vampire's thick boots. *Okay, that hurt.* I circled again, and saw with alarm, three dark specks approaching. *Reinforcements.*

He paused and held his hand against his dark eyes to shield them from the harsh sunlight. A smile broke his serious face. "My friends are coming," Carlos said, looking up at the three dark specks.

And that's when I leaped at his neck, taking advantage of his lapse of concentration. I felt my teeth go around the vampire's neck and then shook with all of my might, letting my wolf instincts take over. With satisfaction, I heard a crack and pop before tumbling onto the ground. I watched as the head rolled away and then turned and ran as fast as I could before Garret, Jesus, and Paul showed up and avenged their now-dead friend.

CHAPTER 16
SAM SILVERTHORN

am," I heard a whisper in the darkness, calling my name. Through my closed eyes, brightness appeared and I felt a little finger tracing the lines of my face. Warmth flooded my head and I could feel something happening. A knitting feeling. My skull had been fractured. I floated between darkness and light.

The pain in my head slowly lessened, and then finally retreated altogether. Now, feeling returned to my body as I felt rocks biting into my back and tasted the metallic taste of blood in my mouth. I must have bitten my tongue.

I blinked and groaned, heaving myself upward. My eyes opened and I saw little Eliana Potentia nearby, the white light still glowing from her fingers.

We were in a cave about twenty feet back. Daylight spilled in from the opening, and Sarah Morris stood in the entrance, her arms crossed, staring at us.

Nearby, my brother Randy leaned against the rock. He looked scared out of his mind and held a rope in his hands. He was passing it through his fingers nervously.

"Now that the little one has healed the werewolf, tie them both up. I can't deal with any more drama today. We've got to get going," Sarah said, glancing over her shoulder out of the cave. "Junior and that vampire are fighting. I wonder who is going to win."

"It's not going to end well," Eliana said, her eyes sad.

There was a pile of rope next to us, and Randy tied Eliana up first. I got up, intending to fight, but Sarah held up her hand, fire at her fingertips. "Werewolves can be killed by fire, and it would be a shame if I had to kill you for the second time in front of your little friend."

I looked down at Eliana, her eyes were big as Randy tied up her hands in front of her. I considered shifting, but then held my hands out obediently as my own brother tied my hands up. In all fairness, he did tie them rather loosely, keeping his eyes on me. "Help her," he mouthed to me while his back was turned to Sarah.

This is interesting, I thought. *Randy has a conscience. Having second thoughts? Well, he always went wherever Junior led him. It's no surprise he got involved in this little attempted coup, but I think this is more than he expected.*

I said nothing and sat down next to Eliana. I put my arms around her in a strange little hug. Listen, I felt a bit of loyalty to Beth. She had been a good partner all these years, and I would protect her daughter with my life if I had to. I thought of Maggie and blinked back tears. She would be worried, and it was cruel of me to turn her into a werewolf. If something happened to me, she would be at the mercy of the pack. If Junior took over, it wouldn't go well for her, and she would probably be exiled from Mt. Storm. *Damn.* This was all so stupid.

"Now, I have to open the gate," Sarah said as she snapped

her fingers. A long sharp wicked knife appeared, and Eliana gasped.

"No!" I said as Eliana buried her head in my chest and started wailing.

"Don't worry. I prefer men for this little ceremony," she said coldly, turning her eyes on Randy.

He screamed and tried to run out of the cave, but she caught him and finished him off in one fell swoop to the neck. I didn't have time to close my eyes. Thankfully, Eliana's face was still buried in my chest, her eyes screwed shut.

I held her tight and rocked her back and forth as my mind processed the terror in front of me. Tears pressed against the back of my eyes as the metallic smell of blood filled the wet cave. Randy didn't deserve this.

My eyes opened again as I held Eliana close to me, seeing my brother laying face-down on the floor. Thankfully, I couldn't see his face, I felt a low moan in my throat rising.

The blood flowed into a puddle, and Sarah began the incantations to open the gate. It appeared behind me, between the pictographs left long ago by the indigenous people who lived here.

It glowed red, and the warmth was almost too hot to bear. Shadows appeared, demons waiting to pour out.

"Don't look. Keep your eyes closed," I mumbled into Eliana's hair, worried that this was all too much for a little girl to witness.

The gate snapped open and Lucifer himself stepped out. I met his gaze and he smirked. "Well, my dear daughter. We finally meet," he said, his voice was rich and warm, and he presented as a handsome man. He was so tall, he towered over us. His long dark hair spilled to his shoulders, wavy, and I could see where little Eliana got her gorgeous locks. His eyes were dark and hard. He wore a red business suit and a white shirt with cufflinks that glinted gold in the red glow from the gate.

Eliana's eyes opened and she lifted her head. "You're not my father!" she said defiantly.

"Ha, ha, ha. I most certainly am," he said, coming close to us. He knelt down and held his arms out wide like he was waiting for a hug. His smell hit my nose and I recoiled. It was an abhorrent combination of brimstone, cologne, and sweaty man. "Come, daughter. It's time to come home."

Eliana withdrew from him, shaking her head back and forth. "No. I won't."

Lucifer paused, biting his lip. Then, he lifted his hand, clenching it into a fist. Instantly, I felt my throat close. I let go of Eliana and clawed at my throat, desperate for air.

"STOP IT!" Eliana screamed. "Don't hurt her!"

"Come with me and I'll let your little doggy friend be," he chuckled, tightening his fist.

The world was going black, pinpricks of light danced in my vision. This was surely the end. Again.

"Fine. I'll come with you," Eliana said, getting to her feet.

Instantly, I could breathe again. I lay on the ground, gasping.

"Boss. Trouble. Potentia Security approaches," Sarah said.

"Go, my minions. Stop her," Lucifer said, waving at the demons, who were all gathered nearby. Instantly, their heads swiveled to the doorway, and their red bodies clambered over each other in the haste to exit.

Lucifer held out his hand to Eliana, and she took it hesitantly, looking back over her shoulder at me.

"Don't worry. She's coming too," Lucifer said in a friendly voice. "Come, Sam. You wouldn't want to leave little Eliana all alone with a monster, would you?"

"You're just going to use me to control her," I said, my eyes flashing. He nodded and snapped his fingers. I was lifted into the air and I hung, helpless.

"Time to go," he said, turning to the hell gate. With a flick of his wrist, I went flying through the gate before him. The world turned black and then red, and I landed with a thump on a particularly hard spot of rock.

"Ouch!" I moaned, rubbing my back. I was going to have to visit a chiropractor when this was all over. My old bones couldn't take it. It was lucky he didn't break my hip.

Lucifer strode through with Eliana, and then I watched as he waved his hand, and the gate opening disappeared. Now, only a smooth rock face remained. We were trapped.

I looked around, we were in a sort of rocky depression in the ground. Red rock cliffs rose all around us and demons climbed up and down the rock faces like monkeys. From above, their insectoid eyes stared down at us and the chittering sound that filled the air made my skin crawl.

In the center of the depression was a large throne. Lucifer walked towards it and Eliana followed obediently.

Shrugging, I followed them both, scanning the area for a way to escape. I could see closed hell gates scattered throughout the area, built into the cliff walls. Several were freestanding, but one could walk through them, just like they were a normal empty door frame.

Lucifer reached his throne and then sat. He snapped his fingers and a huge beast appeared. "This is Toramongus," Lucifer explained, and Eliana and I stared at the ten-foot-tall, dark green named one. He had a lizard-like body with hard skin, scales, and reptilian eyes. A stench, not unlike cow manure, wafted off him.

Eliana said nothing and took a step towards me. I put an arm around her.

"Toramongus. Beth and her gang will be here soon. Any minute now, really. I'm surprised Sarah hasn't come back," he said, rubbing his chin.

As he spoke, Sarah appeared, holding her head. She was soaked and her clothing was charred. She shook her head. "That damn priest and his water gun. Every time."

"Well, now that you're back—" He snapped his fingers, and Sarah returned to normal. She was dry and her clothing appeared undamaged. "You and Toramongus take a horde through the mines. That will keep them distracted while Eliana and I get acquainted."

"Yes, Master," Sarah said, and her and Toramongus, who hissed and slivered just like a snake, moved to a west wall. Lucifer snapped his fingers and the gate glowed red. Demons roared and all moved en masse to flow through the gate.

"You just snap your fingers and the gates open?" Eliana said, her eyes going wide. She looked at me and licked her lips.

"Yes. Come closer, my daughter. Let me get a good look at you." He curled his finger, beckoning to her. I was afraid of what he would do if we didn't comply, so I squeezed her hand and we took a step closer to him.

He leaned forward, his eyes scanning her. He tapped on his chin and then nodded. "You are more like me than your mother, although I see a bit of her in your facial features. Lilith was a good servant. It's too bad she had to die. She wasn't up to snuff to be a named one."

"Is she here?" Eliana whispered, looking at the demons on the rock walls.

"No. She went to limbo. She wasn't a completely evil person, although I do think it's going to take her a very long time to make it upstairs," Lucifer said.

"What do you want with us?" I interrupted as the demons continued to flow through the gate.

"I want nothing to do with you. You are just a little tool to keep my daughter in line." He turned to Eliana. "Dear daughter, you have my powers, don't you see? Together, you and I can finally take over the world. Power, wealth, servants. All will be ours."

"I don't want any of those things. I just want to go to school with my friend, Violet," Eliana said sadly. "Why won't you leave me alone? I didn't ask to be your daughter. I prefer Beth and Dan. They are my real parents."

"Beth Potentia." Lucifer spat in the dirt—his spittle glistened at our feet. "The Potentia line has been a thorn in my side since the beginning of time. Always getting in my way. Do you know their ancestors were thought of as sorcerers? All the kings and queens of Europe hired them and kept me at bay. And then, Horus Potentia had to go and immigrate to America, where he became even more powerful with the US government behind him. Oh, I would love to crush Beth."

"Don't say such things about my mother! I will never join you. You are a bad man!" Eliana said, tears streaming from her eyes. Her face was red and she stomped her foot.

Behind me, the gate shuddered. Toramongus appeared first, a green tuft of hair on the top of his head on fire. Lucifer sighed and snapped his fingers, causing the fire to disappear.

"We don't have long now. Beth will breech the gate any minute. You see, we have been down here for about five minutes, so five weeks have passed in the real world. She's getting desperate."

"Five weeks! I'll miss school!" Eliana wailed.

"I must hide you away. Both of you. She won't be able to find you," he said, his eyes narrowing. "She'll give up, and then I can have all the time I want to bend you to my will."

"Never!" Eliana said, and I put my hand on her shoulder and squeezed gently.

"Bye, bye. I'll see you later," Lucifer said and snapped his fingers.

CHAPTER 17
ESCAPE

There was a blink of darkness and we found ourselves in a room. It wasn't just any room… it was made of red stone. Tapestries covered the wall—vile things—depicting sins of all sorts. An enormous bed was smack dab in the middle of the room, covered with a deep red velvet coverlet.

A fire burned unnecessarily in a fireplace, and a table with black chairs was set for two, with what looked like covered dishes.

A heavy wood door was closed, and I quickly went over to it, trying the ornate iron door handle. *Locked, of course.*

A large glassless window was along the far wall. "Look," Eliana said, stepping over to it.

I went to stand next to her and looked out the window. In the far distance, we could see where we had come from. We were in some type of keep, and we must have been very far up because the stone walls dropped hundreds of feet below me.

Between the keep and where the throne was, pools of lava glowed brightly. Black specks below looked like ants, and I realized they were all demons, moving toward the middle throne.

"It's a battle," I said, straining to see. "And look! It's the Drakes!" Flying through the air, in the far distance, I saw one red dragon and one black dragon. Fire erupted from their mouths, and demons on the ground instantly turned to ash and blew away in the wind.

"They won't be able to find us," Eliana said sadly, leaning out. "Hey, Sam. Look… a way out."

There was a thick stone ledge around this floor. About a foot wide, it was an ornamentation. Interesting, it looked like it led to a balcony.

"Eliana. You healed me back at the cave. Can you do any other magic?" I asked.

She nodded solemnly. "I can do fire. I burned Dr. Gimar accidentally. I apologized though," she added hastily. "I don't like to use it. It's dangerous."

"Do you think you could do that thing Lucifer does and open a gate? I asked.

She cocked her head, thinking for a moment. "Yeah, I think I could."

"Eliana. I'm going to try something. You stay here," I said as I let myself shift into my wolf form.

"You're a very pretty wolf," Eliana said, smiling. I stood, my silver fur shining, and then hopped up on the windowsill. I wanted to be in my wolf form because, in this body, my balance was superb, my eyesight sharp, and my fangs and claws a formable tool. My wolf body was much more reliable than my old lady body.

I easily padded down the stone ledge. Reaching the balcony, I scrambled over the rail. It looked like some kind of library niche. Books lined the wall, all written in some kind of indecipherable runes. More importantly was that it opened up into a large hall, and I could see a staircase that went down.

Retracing my steps, I returned to Eliana.

"Is it safe?" she asked. I nodded my wolf head and she scrambled out on the ledge.

I was afraid she would tumble to her death or become too scared to move forward, but I had to give it to that little girl… she set her eyes forward, and put one foot in front of the other, with just her left hand trailing lightly on the wall.

In seconds, she scrambled over the railing to the balcony and entered the library area. She stopped for a moment, staring at the books. "I can read them," she whispered as she stood staring at the dark leather bindings. "Dark Magic, Blood Rites, Demon Possession."

I jerked my head, not wanting to turn back into my human form. She followed me down the hallway, which was empty and as quiet as a church.

In fact, my keen wolf hearing picked up no sound. Not even rodents in the walls. Everyone was gone, perhaps to fight the battle.

This castle was exquisitely decorated. It was like all the Ann Rice fans descended on this castle with a Visa Platinum credit card and had their way with the draperies. Heavy velvet, thick rugs, jewel tones, and dark metals covered every surface.

We stumbled on the first demon and both Eliana and I nearly jumped out of our skin. He was carrying a bunch of firewood across his scrawny red back, and he paid us no mind, continuing on.

As we went down another level, we passed two demons carrying pails, buckets, and mops. Apparently, here, the demons were used as servants.

No one seemed concerned about us, so I shifted back into my

human form. As I did, I felt my cell phone in my pocket. On a whim, I pulled it out. It was black. I tried to turn it on—nothing. Apparently, cell phones didn't work in hell.

We reached the main level, and here, a long hallway stretched farther than we could see. "Look." I breathed a sigh of relief. "Gates."

"They are all closed," Eliana said, "And my mother said that every gate in hell leads to a spot on earth. How do we know where it goes? What if we come out in China?"

I shook my head. "You know something else I'm worried about? The time difference. Every minute we stay here, a week passes on the outside. Or so I'm told."

"My mom will be so worried about me. How long have we been in here?" Eliana asked, her eyes looking down the hall.

"I'm not sure. It feels like we haven't been here that long, but my phone is dead and I haven't seen any clocks."

We walked down the long hallway, looking up at the elaborately carved gates. Runes were engraved into the dark rocks.

"Can you read that?" I asked, pointing up at the lintel.

"Oh, yeah! It says Germany," Eliana said brightly.

"So, I guess it tells us where we are going to go?" I said, a smile coming to my face.

"Yeah!" she said, and we walked down the hallway, hand in hand, reading the lintels. "France, Spain, Russia…"

"Hey. What are you doing out of your room? The Master will be angry," a voice broke our study of the doors.

I looked up, startled. He was a large purple demon with long corkscrew horns that hung down past his chin. His eyes were yellow and narrowed at us. Luckily, he was far down the hall.

"It's a named one," I whispered to Eliana. "Open a gate."

She looked around desperately. All the gates near us were nowhere near North America.

"That's right! I am a named one. Eldrichas is the most powerful named one. MASTER!" he shouted, and the word seemed to vibrate through the very stone. "They are escaping!"

The keep around us was beginning to vibrate. Eliana spun around in a circle, her eyes wild as she trembled.

Eldrichas took a step forward and the ground shook. "Eliana. Try to open a gate! Any gate!" I pleaded.

She stopped and turned toward the nearest gate. She was trembling and she stared at it intently as if she was reaching deep inside her. She took a deep breath and tried to snap her fingers. Nothing happened.

"It's not working. Before, when I closed a gate, I just thought about it and it worked!" she wailed and then threw a harried look behind her shoulder. Eldrichas was slow, and each step felt like he was walking in thick mud. Her face went pale, and she tried again to snap her fingers.

I moved in front of her, shielding her with my body. "Eliana. Please hurry!" I said, holding my hand up in front of my face. I snapped my fingers. Once, twice, three times, demonstrating.

She tried again, staring at the gate. She licked her lips and I could almost see sweat forming on her head.

Desperate, I threw a suggestion out there. "Slowly. Do it slowly and carefully!" I pleaded.

She tossed her black hair and took a deep breath. She held her hand up. Eldrichas was just ten steps away from us now. Suddenly, her thumb and forefinger made a snapping sound, and the gateway blazed to life.

I took Eliana's hand. Through the gate, I could see a busy street, people with brown skin, riding bikes and mopeds down what looked like a bright day. "Let's go," I said, my voice raising.

"Eliana! Nooooo!" a voice yelled down the hallway. We turned and saw Lucifer stood there, in his demon form, his red chest heaving.

Without a moment's hesitation, we jumped through the gate, holding each other's hands tightly.

CHAPTER 18
MUMBAI

We stepped out into some sort of cave, hewn out of a dark rock. The gate glowed behind us. I took a few steps toward the entrance and saw an approaching group of children. It looked like a school group, but wherever we were, it wasn't the United States. The brown-skinned children all wore school uniforms with a white button-up top and a navy striped tie. The girls wore pleated skirts with their black hair pulled back in ponytails, and the boys all wore what could only be described as dress shorts. The children were led by a stern-looking teacher wearing a yellow sari.

I took stock and realized we made a strange sight. Two Westerners, standing in the middle of a foreign land like they had been dropped here out of the blue. "Where are we?" I asked Eliana.

"The gate said India," Eliana whispered, her eyes wide.

The walls of the cave were decorated with ancient carvings. "Eliana, the gate!" I said, urgency creeping into my voice as the school group approached.

She turned and tried to snap again, getting it on the third try. I breathed a sigh of relief as the glow disappeared.

"Who are you? You came out of the hell gate?" a trembling voice spoke English out of the shadows. He was a young Indian man, wearing a white linen shirt and pants. He was holding a wand firmly in his hand, and his eyes were wide and scared.

I held up my hands, "We mean no harm. This is Eliana Potentia, and I am her protector, Sam Silverthorn. We need your help. First, where are we?"

He furtively looked left and right as the school group approached the entrance. "You are in Mumbai, at the Mahakali Caves. It's an ancient site that also conceals a secret gate to the underworld. Hurry, we must leave. This site needs to be shut down for the day."

We followed him cautiously out of the cave opening and encountered the school group, preparing to enter. They cast us Westerners curious glances, and the smaller children whispered to each other.

"I'm so sorry, the caves must be closed for the day," our guide said, shaking his head sadly. "A large stone fell from the ceiling, so we must make sure it's safe for visitors."

The teacher's face turned red, and she threw up her hands in disgust, "What do you mean, closed? This trip has been planned for months! This is part of our lessons."

"I understand. You can reschedule your trip when it's safe," our guide said. The school children then made their way back to a unique yellow school bus parked on the corner. It looked not much larger than a Volkswagen bus at home, and the children climbed in, crowding the aisle. They grinned and waved at us, speaking a mixture of their native language and English.

As they pulled away, our guide glanced quickly back at the caves. "My name is Aditya Patel. Please, come with me, I work for Mumbai Security. We know Beth Potentia and she's put out an all-points bulletin for you two around the world. I never expected you two to fall out of my hell gate." He looked worried and took yet another glance back at the structure before pulling out a cell phone and speaking urgently in his native tongue.

I noticed how hot it was as we walked out of the cave. The heat hit us, and I was instantly covered with a sheen of sweat. With the air outside that smelled like vehicle exhaust, it was suffocating, and the high humidity gave everything a haze.

A horn honked shrilly, and an auto rickshaw swerved around us with unintelligible yelling. We were standing in the middle of a very busy street. To the right of us, three reddish-brown, skinny cows lay in a spot of shade in a pile of plastic and paper garbage.

"Sam! Why are there cows in the middle of the city?" Eliana asked, tugging on my sleeve.

Honestly, I had no idea. I vaguely remembered something about cows being important in Hindi religion. I opened my mouth to tell her this, but our new friend, Aditya, interrupted.

"In India, our cows are sacred. The animals roam unharmed. People and traffic just move around them. Our Hindu religion holds cows in reverence because they are believed to contain our ancestors' souls," he said, shoving his cell phone back in his pocket.

"That's so interesting!" Eliana said, her eyes wide. "Father Burke said we should respect all religions and people because it takes all types to make the world turn."

Aditya's eyes sparkled. "Yes, that is a good outlook. Now, you must come with me to the office. My boss will put you in contact with your people."

"Let's go then… the sooner the better," I said, pulling Eliana through the traffic. We followed Aditya, and he replaced his wand on his belt as he strode confidently forward. We turned a corner and it became more congested. The buildings were narrow, gray, and had signs in both Hindi and English. We passed a street market, fragrant with piles of chilis, tamarind pods, ginger root knobs, and curry powder. The carts were covered with various colors of torn and faded umbrellas, and women in purple, red, and green saris moved through the crowds with shopping bags full of their daily grocery shopping.

Now, a stream of motorbikes crossed in front of us, and I was afraid for my life. Aditya just walked into the street and then glanced back. "Don't be afraid, just follow me. It's down this way. Not far at all."

I gulped and took Eliana's hand in mine. She gripped my hand tighter than one would expect a small child to grip it. We started forward, our eyes firmly on Aditya's back.

Finally, we reached the other side of the busy street. We followed our new friend down the sidewalk. Now, we were in a more commercial area. The stench of back alleys and trash replaced the market smells from before.

A big modern-looking building loomed above us. It was four stories high, and its glass and bright white concrete shone in the patchwork collection of local businesses that lined the street.

"Mumbai Security," he said, gesturing toward the building, and I pulled Eliana along, hoping that we could be in contact with our friends soon.

CHAPTER 19
SECURITY

We walked up several steps and into the building. A gust of icy air conditioning hit me, and I nearly gasped from the heat difference.

A receptionist sat in the middle of the white hall. He wore all black and made a striking figure.

He looked up and a smile crossed his face. "Welcome to Mumbai Security. Here, I've prepared passes for you." He handed them over, and Aditya took an ID out of his pocket and clipped it on his linen shirt.

Eliana held hers up and inspected it closely, then she put the lanyard around her neck. It hung to her waist. "Cool. I feel like a grown-up. Mom should get some of these."

I stifled a giggle, "We have a bit of a different setup in Mt. Storm. Everyone knows everyone else, and if they don't know exactly what Potentia Security does on the top of the mountain, they sure know we ain't what we seem to be."

"You have a wonderful accent," the receptionist said in a lilt I had only heard on television.

"As do you," I smiled, and Aditya moved us to the elevator,

where he swiped his key card at a sensor to get in. We moved up to the fourth floor and the elevator opened. A long hall with desks, terminals, and a half-dozen people all turned to look at us.

A tall woman wearing a jade green sari quickly got up from a large table at the end of the hall and moved forward, beaming. "Welcome! I'm Divya Patel, head of Mumbai Security. Sam, Eliana. A pleasure to host you. I can't believe that you found one of our gates to come through! Everyone has been looking for you!"

"How long have we been gone?" I asked, my brow furrowing.

"Ten weeks," she said with a frown. "And Beth Potentia has been frantic."

"Oh no! I missed Christmas." Eliana's face fell and I realized her school year was probably almost over.

"I'm sure Santa still left you presents," I said, looking down at her crestfallen face.

She tilted her head. "Do you think so?"

"I'm sure of it," I smiled and then turned my attention back to Divya Patel.

"Please, have a seat. We have already contacted Potentia Security, and they are most anxious to speak to you. There is a nine-hour time difference, so it is still very early in West Virginia. Why don't I introduce the team to you while we wait for the video call," Divya suggested, taking a seat in one of the white leather swivel chairs.

Aditya sat down to her right side and we were joined by two more people.

"This is our staff that is on duty right now. We have twenty magical users and shape-shifters like yourself. Sam, you'll be interested to know my friend, Kabir, here is a Yaksha… or werewolf."

My eyes widened and I turned to him. He smiled at me and ran a hand over his shortcut mustache. "Welcome. It is a pleasure to meet an American werewolf. There is much the same, yet much different, about our packs."

"I am the leader of my pack in West Virginia. The Silverthorns go back hundreds of years," I said, giving him a respectful nod. "You are welcome at our fire any time, friend."

He looked a little shocked. "You are the leader? I would love to know more about the Silverthorns."

"Some other time, Kabir," the woman next to him said. She was thin and had a crafty look about her. "I am Charita. A naga. I have the power to turn into a snake."

"A snake! Do you bite?" Eliana asked, her eyes widened, and she inched closer to me.

"Only people I don't like," she said darkly, narrowing her eyes, but then she smiled. "Don't worry, little one. I don't bite little girls."

"I have tasked my team to look after you while you are here. There have been some complications," Divya said, clasping her hands together in front of her.

"What has happened?" I asked, looking down the table at the team.

Just then, a large screen hanging on the wall blinked on. A green light appeared at the top of the screen and Beth Potentia's tired face filled it. I could see she was at the conference table in Mt. Storm. Her husband, Dan, Easton, Garret, and Father Burke were sitting with her.

"Mom!" Eliana said, bouncing in her seat. "We went through! It was really scary, and my father… I mean, not Dan, locked us in a tower."

Beth's eyes filled with tears and she burst into sobs. Dan reached over and gave her a hug, then turned to the camera. "And my smart girl escaped. If he hurt you…"

I interrupted him mid-rant. "We are fine, Dan. Eliana used her magic, and we opened a random portal we found. Unfortunately, we ended up here in Mumbai. Luckily, we ran into these wonderful people who have helped us out."

Beth wiped her eyes. Her face was red and splotchy. "Thank you, Sam. Thank you so much. I don't know how I can ever repay you. I'm sorry to tell you this, but your brother, Randy, is dead."

It felt like I had been punched in the gut. I blinked and sat in shock for a moment. Finally, the words came to me. "He was injured badly. I hoped he had made it. I'll take care of all of that when I get back. How is Maggie?"

"She's a nervous wreck. I had to explain to her a lot more than I intended. When I heard, I called her right away, and it was everything I could do to keep her from hopping on a plane to Mumbai," Beth laughed. "Maggie promised to let me work."

I smiled. "Good luck with that."

"Listen, we have to talk about getting you two back. It's not as easy as it sounds," Beth said, tapping on her papers.

Easton turned his serious face to the video camera, his sunglasses were off for a change, and his dark brown eyes were filled with concern. "The President is furious. She's making threats. She said that if Eliana returns, she's not living in Mt. Storm anymore. Which is ridiculous."

"What! I can't live with my family?" Eliana's face twisted in pain. "Mt. Storm is my home! Where am I supposed to live?"

Beth bit her lip. "She wants you to live at the NSA with Dr. Gimar."

"Absolutely not. You tell Madame President to stuff it," Dan said, banging on the table. Obviously, this was the first he was hearing of this.

"So, we have two choices. Eliana can stay in India, or some other friendly country with Sam until she can safely come home, or…"

"NO! I want to come home!" Eliana said, her eyes filling with tears. They ran down her face. "Why does Madame President have to be so mean?"

"The other option is that you come home and we protect and hide you here," Beth said, looking around her team.

"Why do you seem nervous about that one?" I asked, observing her face on the screen.

She turned to me and looked over to Dan. "We can't use our normal plane. I have to arrange that through the government. Flying commercial is just as dangerous."

"So, that leaves a boat," I said. But surely the government could easily figure out what boat we were on and stop us at customs. Not to mention neither Eliana nor I had a passport with us.

"There is one other way," Beth said, looking at her team.

"Limbo," Divya guessed, her eyes lighting up with delight.

"Bingo. But it won't be easy. You'll have to use your contacts there," Beth said, worry creasing her forehead.

Divya clapped her hands and looked toward her team. "We need to contact the Indian government and plan to open the gate to Limbo. With utmost discretion, of course. No mention of our guests here."

"Of course," Charita said, scribbling a note, a little smile on her face. "I'll start calling today. The head of the National Technical Research Organization is an old friend of mine."

After the meeting, Divya took us into her office. It was decorated in a modern style, with pops of color on the chairs. A tropical plant was in the corner and a large whiteboard covered the wall.

"It may be a few weeks before the time is right to go to Limbo," she said. "We need to figure out where you will stay."

"Can we stay at a hotel or something?" I asked, settling back into the comfortable chair. Eliana sat beside me, taking it all in.

"I want you protected. I have an idea," she said and leaned over and picked up her phone. She dialed an extension and then spoke briskly. "Kabir, would you be willing to host our guests? You and your family can protect them should trouble arise."

She listened for a moment, arranging details before hanging up, and then Kabir came around the corner, grinning. "I am most pleased to host our esteemed guests. I have called my wife, and she is preparing a feast. Little one, you will be pleased I have many children who will be happy to make a new friend."

I smiled and leaned forward. "Thank you. That sounds lovely. Do you live here in the city?"

"No, we prefer wild places. The only spot left here in Mumbai that is wild is the Sanjay Gandhi National Park. We have a special disposition from the Prime Minister that allows us to live in the park. We are tucked away, safe, and we help patrol the park for Mumbai Security. My family is an important safeguard for the citizens of India."

"How do we get there?" Eliana asked, her eyes bright. "Are we going to take one of those funny buses?"

"No, we will take a motorbike. I've called one of my brothers to bring another one. I've asked him to come at the end of the workday."

"Until then, we need to take you to purchase some clothing. Big Bazaar is a large store where you can find almost anything."

"Beth has approved emergency funding for you two," Divya added. She opened her desk drawer and took out an envelope of cash. She looked inside and then slid the envelope to me. "That's 30,000 Indian Rupees."

"Thank you," I said, noting that the bank notes were as brightly colored as everything else. Purple, green, orange, and yellow notes, all with Gandhi's smiling face.

We left soon afterwards with our guide. Kabir hailed an auto rickshaw, its body green and yellow. I looked dubiously at it. The open doors and small body didn't seem like we would all fit.

"I'll sit in the front." Kabir smiled, and the driver looked at us with a huge grin, then said something in the native language, waving toward the back.

Eliana and I cautiously sat on the vinyl seats, and the rickshaw zoomed through the traffic. Several times, I screwed my eyes shut. This was not for the faint of heart.

We arrived at our destination and went inside. It was strangely like one of our big box stores, with Western-style clothing with an Indian twist. I grabbed a shopping cart, feeling out of place. The locals stared at me strangely. I'm sure with my short silver hair and white skin, I looked like I had just wandered out of the circus.

We quickly picked out some basics. Clothing, toiletries, and a duffle bag to shove it all in. I picked up a cell phone, a sim card, and an international plan. As soon as the phone was activated, I paid for everything with some of the brightly-colored money, then headed back out.

When we got back, we sat in the staff cafeteria. A man came in, loaded with stainless steel lunch boxes. A fragrant smell of curry filled the room. He passed one out to every employee, and we were delighted when he had one for us. "Divya called and told us to add two for Westerners. I wasn't sure what your taste buds would enjoy, so I tried to pick out something most tourists to India like," the server said, passing us two tall lunch box cylinders.

We opened them carefully, watching Kabir. "This is Aloo Gobi with rice and roti," he said, folding his napkin on his lap carefully.

I dug in as my stomach growled and my mouth watered. The lunchroom was fragrant with the heady smell of Indian spices, and the heat in my mouth built. Eliana hesitantly tried her dish and settled on eating just the rice and roti. I smiled as I gulped down a bottle of water. This was definitely a cultural experience she would not forget.

After we ate lunch, we stayed in the break room. Eliana watched the television on the wall. An animated show called Sally Bollywood came on, featuring a young Indian girl who solved crime. I watched it for a few minutes, then turned to my cell phone, eager to call Maggie.

I looked at the clock and noted it was 4 o'clock in the afternoon now. Doing quick math, I realized it would be about 7 am in West Virginia. Maggie was an early riser, and would already be up, probably anxiously awaiting news.

I dialed her number and she answered on the first ring. "Maggie. I'm sorry," I said before she could even get a word out.

On the phone, she burst into tears. "Sam! I thought you were dead, lost, or hurt. They found Randy dead, and Junior wasn't talking. Beth assured me you and Eliana must have gone through the portal. I just hoped against hope you were still alive. I've been so worried."

"I love you so much," I said, running my hand through my silver hair. "It's only been a day for me, but I know to you it's been a long time."

"It's been ten weeks and in that time, your brother has been perfectly awful to me. He's out on bail again. Chad Duchamp got him out. But, Sam, Buster came by… he said you owe him a lot of money."

I winced as my stomach sank. "I sort of forgot about all that. Buster will be my next call. He's got to be livid."

"He said if he doesn't get his money, he's going to curse us. What does that mean?" Maggie asked. In my mind's eye, I could see her at our kitchen table, fretting over leprechauns, werewolves, and the bills I had left stacked there.

"Don't worry about it. I'll take care of it," I assured her. "The only problem is, I don't know when we can get home. It's complicated." I looked over at Eliana. She was intently watching the show from the sofa, her knees pulled to her chin.

"Why can't you just get on a plane?" Maggie asked, her voice quivering. "I need you here. I restarted up the salon, but it's been slow. Not only did I lose the old customers, but the younger ones are also going to that new salon in the strip mall. The owner is really nice. She's young and specializes in a lot of the current styles. Bright dye jobs, shaved mohawks, Brazilian blowouts… that kind of thing." I heard the sadness in Maggie's voice.

"Your bread and butter has always been the curl and sets," I said, thinking that she had inherited most of Cindy Potentia's customers when the business was sold. It was dated with old-fashioned chairs and decor. Nothing about The Clip and Cut screamed modern or punk.

"Yeah, but it's just not working," she said, sounding miserable. "I started it up again because I was afraid you weren't coming back. Maybe I need to turn the keys to the building over to Buster to help pay off the debt."

"Absolutely not," I said. "We will think of something. If

Buster doesn't curse us forever, I want to get the whiskey business set up."

Eliana looked over at me and then yawned. It had been a long, strange day for both of us.

"I have faith," Maggie said. "I miss you, babe."

"Same. Listen, I'm going to be staying with some Indian werewolves tonight. Now that I've got this cell phone, call me any time. Just remember the time difference."

"Of course. I think I can face the day now, knowing you're alright," Maggie said, and I blew her a kiss across the phone lines.

After I hung up, I sighed deeply, looked up the number for Mt. Storm Motors, and made the call. I had to get Buster off my back.

Unfortunately, he didn't answer. I was hoping for at least a voicemail, but it just rang and rang. With a sigh, I put my new cell phone back in my pocket. I guess that was a problem for another day.

CHAPTER 20
BONDS

The dense foliage of the Sanjay Gandhi National Forest was awash with the golden glow of the setting sun, and the trees danced in the last light of the day. The distant hustle and bustle of Mumbai felt worlds away, here in this cool oasis.

Kabir, with a confident stride, led us through an unmarked trail. The scent of wet earth filled the air. I felt as if we were venturing into a sacred enclave. Eliana stayed close to me, clutching my hand tightly.

"I've always been curious about werewolf packs in other parts of the world," I remarked, looking right and left through the leaves.

Kabir grinned, his eyes taking on a mischievous glint in the fading light. "Every pack is unique. I've been all over India, and even here, our packs vary wildly."

Eliana's grip tightened around my hand, and she whispered, "Will they like me, Sam?"

I bent down and locked eyes with Eliana. "Of course, they

will. And remember, you're with me. There's nothing to be afraid of. Think of it as a school field trip."

The rhythmic beat of Bollywood music reached our ears, and we entered a large clearing. Small rough houses stood at one end, and its center was a roaring bonfire, casting flickering firelight on the people surrounding it. A small radio by the fire seemed to sit in a place of prominence, and a card table was filled with a wide selection of dishes. It was pack dinner time, and the familiarity of it caused me to smile.

The Indian werewolves, in their human forms, were a diverse lot. They varied from young to old, and their attire was a blend of modern and traditional. Many wore kurtas and jeans, while others sported t-shirts with popular Indian movie stars.

"That's Indu," Kabir said, pointing out the pack's leader with flowing black hair adorned with jasmine flowers.

She noticed us and approached with a welcoming smile. "Welcome, Sam Silverthorn. You honor us with your presence." Her gaze then softened as she looked at Eliana. "And this must be the young one. Namaste, Eliana."

Eliana gave her a shy smile, staying close to my side. "Namaste."

"Please, come and join us for our pack night. You are a welcomed guest," Indu said, leading us over to a few empty folding chairs. I sat down carefully, and instead of taking an empty chair, Eliana sat on my lap, her dark eyes taking everything in.

It was so familiar, I could close my eyes and feel at home, but there were things that jolted me out of that daydream. One, the spicy aroma of food being prepared. At home, we would have some sort of game and vegetables from the gardens. Here, colorful lanterns replaced our Coleman camping lanterns and mosquito candles. Their soft, colorful glow illuminated the area.

At home, country music by Luke Combs or Tim McGraw would be playing. But here, the energetic Bollywood beats gave a completely different vibe.

And, unlike our pack night, which was filled with drama and problems, their pack night was a simple listing of chores and jobs. It seemed like many of these werewolves worked for Mumbai Security in the field. There was no worry about money, and everyone seemed content.

As the evening deepened, it turned more into a social event. Stories were told, and a glass bottle of clear liquid was passed around. As it came to me, I chuckled. "Even in India, you make your own spirits."

Indu smiled, "It is mahua. We brew it ourselves proudly. For years, the British banned the drink, but we still brewed it. It's made with the flowers of the mahua tree."

I took another sip. It was nothing like anything I had ever tasted. "If I could, I would share with you a bottle of Silverthorn Moonshine. You'll have to visit us one day."

Eliana was staring at the woman, and she said shyly, "The designs on your hands are so beautiful. Are they tattoos?"

"No, it's called henna. Each design tells a tale, and they are a type of decoration. Would you like your own design?" Indu asked gently. "It's not permanent."

Eliana looked up at me with pleading eyes, and I nodded, then watched as Indu called for one of the women to come with a paintbrush and a pot of what looked like a green clay. She painted a floral design on the back of Eliana's hand. Eliana was delighted.

The night grew darker, and the full moon ascended, illuminating the forest. I looked up, feeling a primal pull in my gut. The call of the moon was strong, and I knew at home in West Virginia, my pack would be out, patrolling the land and hunting in the moonlight. The urge grew stronger, and I pulled my knees up to my chest, looking down at my dusty running shoes.

Indu looked over at me. "The urge is primal. You must miss your home."

"Yes. I do. I miss my partner and my family."

"The need to hunt, to feel the earth between your paws… I know this longing. I went to university in New Delhi. It was hard for me to get out of nature. Why don't you go out with my pack? I'll wait here with a few others with the little one. We will protect her. No demon would dare set foot on these lands."

I looked over at Eliana, who was now sitting in the dirt, rolling small matchbox cars with two of the smaller boys. She looked up at me and smiled, the henna still fresh on her hand. The silvery moonlight shone down on her, and my itch to shift grew stronger. "She is my responsibility. I worry about her."

Indu placed a reassuring hand on my shoulder. "Our pack will protect her as if she is our own. She's safe here."

Taking a deep breath, I nodded, my concern easing. Of course, they would protect her, just as my pack would protect a guest. "Thank you, Indu."

"Besides, as part of our patrol, we will check known gates. You can see for yourself they are still closed," Indu said, picking up a bowl of a light Indian crackers and delicately picking out two and popping them in her mouth.

With a last glance toward Eliana, who was now engrossed with her new friends, building a road with sticks and rocks for the cars, I retreated to a secluded part of the clearing to shift. It was quick, my form shifting fluidly from human to wolf. My silvery coat gleamed in the moonlight as I bounded into the forest, surrendering to the call of the wild.

I was joined by several other wolves with dark fur. The one

next to me was large, and when he howled in greeting, I recognized Kabir, who touched noses with me, and then took off through the underbrush. Following, I lifted my nose, adding my voice to this new pack.

The hunt was exhilarating. The scents of the forest, the rush of the wind against my fur, the thrill of the chase. For those few hours, I was a member of this pack. We hunted a cheetah, which seemed dangerous to me, but we did not catch it. Instead, we chased it far north.

Looping back to the clearing with Kabir and his friends, I was panting but content. I found Eliana asleep in a rope hammock. She had been covered with a light blanket, cocooned in the protective embrace of the pack. Indu sat nearby, keeping a careful watch by the dying embers of the fire.

"She missed you," Indu remarked softly as I approached. "But she knew you'd return. She's a strong one."

Along with the others, I transformed back to my human form and smiled gratefully. "Thank you, Indu. Tonight was a gift. I will never forget it."

An understanding passed between us. Indu nodded and then shifted herself, disappearing into the trees with several of her pack mates. I wondered if they would hunt cheetahs again, or perhaps the spotted deer I had only glimpsed.

Kabir approached me. "You can sleep with my family. Our shelter is tight but cozy. We have sleeping pads and more blankets."

Gently, with the utmost care, I picked up Eliana from the hammock in my arms. Her face was relaxed, her breaths even and rhythmic. I felt motherly feelings I had pushed down in my youth. A little pang, a wish that maybe I should have had a few pups of my own. Then I shook that thought out of my head. At fifty, that ship had long sailed.

Walking toward the makeshift shelters at the edge of the clearing, I could feel the eyes of the pack on us—not in scrutiny, but in protection. The simple structures were constructed of plywood with tin roofs. A blanket hung over the opening. Inside, mats lined the floor. Kabir pointed to a spot between several of his children.

Setting Eliana down onto the padding and then covering her with a spare blanket, I took a moment to simply watch her. Brushing a stray hair from her face, she smiled in her sleep and then curled up on her side.

Through the doorway, I heard crickets. The night was thick with warmth, Mumbai's tropical air wrapping around us like a blanket. If I closed my eyes, I could imagine I was in West Virginia, maybe camping with my brothers. I nestled close to Eliana and pulled a thin blanket over my shoulder as I tried to find sleep.

Outside the shelter, the Indian werewolf pack settled in their own spaces, yet their collective presence surrounded us. Every so often, a soft howl or murmur would break the silence. I felt safe here.

Kabir took a spot just outside the shelter's door, shifting into a werewolf and crouching, alert and on guard. He was illuminated by the soft moonlight, keeping a watchful eye, ensuring that we were all safe.

My breathing slowed and I felt myself drifting off to sleep. My body grew heavy, and as I drifted off, I heard Indu's voice.

"The gates are still closed. It looks like they are safe, for now."

CHAPTER 21
AN UNEXPECTED INVITATION

sat up the next morning, every bone in my old body aching. I wasn't meant to sleep on the floor. I must have looked terrible because Kabir's wife, who was much younger, offered me a hand up.

"Turmeric tea is what you need," she tutted. "That's what we give our elders."

"Elders! I'm only 50!" I said, horrified. Stretching slightly, I looked around for Eliana.

"She's with the other children. They are already playing, it being a Saturday. No school," Kabir's wife chirped, pouring me a glass of tea from a steaming pot on a nearby hot plate.

I took it, blowing on the top. It was fragrant, and I could taste the turmeric. *Well*, I thought, *maybe it will help.*

I stumbled outside with a change of clothes and found the privy. Wrinkling my nose, I thanked the lord above for indoor plumbing at home.

Finding the central fire, I found Kabir crouched down with two other men. He looked up as I approached and handed me a foil-wrapped pack. "Some warm roti."

I took the pack, sitting on a nearby chair, balancing my mug of tea on my knee. "What's the plan?" I asked, then took a big bite of the bread. It was still warm and buttery. It wasn't Dunn's Donuts, but it was pretty good.

"You two will travel to New Delhi today. Divya has been in contact with the Prime Minister," Kabir said, poking the fire with a stick. He looked at me, concern on his face.

"Well, that was fast," I said, taking another sip of my tea. It might have just been a placebo effect, but I felt more sprightly. I looked around for Eliana. She was playing happily with the other children, running through the underbrush, leaves in her hair.

"I'll come with you, of course. Divya has tasked me with being your handler the rest of the time you are in India. We will get you home. Don't worry."

"Thank you, Kabir. You have been most kind. I hope sometime I can return the hospitality," I said, thinking the past few days had been insane. What I wouldn't give to just have a few minutes to figure out my own problems.

We weren't really sure when the government officials would show up, so we spent a quiet morning nearby. At noon, we were served a simple meal of rice, more roti, and a curry lentil dish. The day grew hot and sticky, and everyone found shade to relax in.

Eliana used my phone to speak to Beth and Dan, and even Violet, her eyes lighting up when she told her about our little adventure. Then, her and the other children played the Indian version of hide and seek.

Turning to my own business, I reclaimed the phone. It was time to work out the pack problems. Junior wouldn't take my calls, but my brothers, Frankie and Dennis, brought me up to speed with everything that had happened while I was gone.

I encouraged them to look around for a space we could use, and to make some inquiries about getting the proper licenses. Alarmingly, they had seen Buster around a few times. He would come into the auto shop, look around with a smirk, and then leave. I was getting worried.

Wandering into the hut where we slept, I packed up the few things we had bought and put the bag by the door. The hut was empty, so I sat with my legs crossed on the mat. Outside, the women were prepping the evening meal. I picked up my cell phone, turning on the power again. I would need to plug it into the generator soon. I only had a few bars left. Maggie's voice echoed across the vast distance, filled with relief to hear my voice.

"When do you think you'll be back? I miss you so much. It doesn't seem fair. We were just married, and you've been missing for months!" Maggie said. I imagined our voices traveling at the speed of light.

"I don't quite understand the science, but it has something to do with gates being aligned properly in Limbo. We also need permission from the government, which Indu doesn't seem to think is going to be a problem, but you never know."

"Why can't you just get on the plane?" Maggie asked again, her voice sounding desperate. In the background, I heard the door jingle. I heard her greet her customer, and then her harried voice came back on the line. "It's Mrs. Peterson. She's a half an hour early for her appointment."

"Going through the gate is our ticket back to West Virginia. Given the situation with Eliana, I'm told it's the safest route," I said. Talking it out with Maggie seemed to calm my nerves, somehow.

"I'll be with you in just a minute, Mrs. Peterson," Maggie said, and then her voice lowered to a whisper. "Beth came by yesterday. She said the president has demanded Eliana be returned to the NSA. They will hold her indefinitely. Sam, promise me you'll protect her."

I looked out the door again and Eliana was spinning around in circles, holding hands with one of Kabir's daughters. Their voices were filled with joy, and then they tumbled to the ground together, giggling.

"I promise. I won't let anything happen to her. We're close, Maggie. We'll be home before you know it."

"I've got to go. Mrs. Peterson is scowling at me," she whispered. "Love you, babe."

With a sigh, I ended the call and leaned back against the rough wall, then I got up, my knee popping loudly. If I didn't get back to my bed soon, I was going to fall apart piece by piece. *Dang my old knees.* I grabbed our bag and walked out, sitting down next to Kabir.

The jovial mood abruptly ended when the group of officials we had been waiting for all morning appeared from the path. They were dressed impeccably in Indian police outfits, khaki colored with olive hats. The group was stern-faced, and they immediately approached Kabir and Indu, who met them head-on, engaging in quiet conversation before turning toward me and calling me forward.

The leading figure, a poised woman with an air of authority, introduced herself. "I'm Special Envoy Mehta. I come with an invitation from the Prime Minister of India. There's been much discussion about the Limbo gate you seek to use."

I frowned. "We were told it was secure. We need to use the gate to return home safely. The alignment is our only shot at bypassing the US authorities without complications."

Indu touched my arm. "You can use the gate. But the Prime Minister would like to meet you first."

I let out a deep sigh and nodded wearily. Eliana, sensing the gravity, clutched my hand. We were so close to going home, but we had to meet yet another official. Already, I felt weary at the thought of playing the part.

I glanced over at my new friends. I grabbed our bag and stood. "Alright. Let's meet and sort this out."

CHAPTER 22
AUDIENCE

We walked through the woods, an odd collection. We neared the trailhead and found a few official-looking vehicles waiting for us. Kabir and Indu were apparently going with us, and we all climbed into several vehicles, then they whisked us off before we could blink.

We drove through the city streets faster than I would have thought possible. The bikes and rickshaws parting in front of us so we could pass. The dense cityscape seemed to hug us close, and I realized I might never see Mumbai again. I would have never thought a girl from the backwoods of West Virginia, a moonshiner's daughter, would visit India.

I blinked as we approached an airport gate and were waved through. The policeman sitting next to the driver turned around. "We are going to be taking a helicopter. It's quite a long journey by car to the capital."

"A helicopter! Cool!" Eliana said, her eyes going wide. In fact, a large military helicopter was waiting for us, its tan paint stark against the bright blue skies. The helicopter blades rhythmically beat the air. I could feel the thump of it in my chest.

We ran to the open door, dunking as instructed. Kabir and Indu waved us goodbye and Eliana and I breathlessly took our seats.

The captain turned around in his seat, giving us a thumbs-up. The co-pilot passed out headphones and then began speaking into our ears.

"Welcome aboard. We will be in New Delhi in about two hours. We will land directly at the Prime Minister's residence. I wanted to let you know you will stay the night as honored guests."

"Thank you," I said into the little mic, then turned to the window. The dense cityscape grew smaller as we ascended into the air, and the constant hum of the helicopter blades prevented much talking. To the west, I saw the Arabian Sea, the sun a glowing orange globe in the sky.

Eliana's eyes sparkled with excitement as she pressed her face against the window, gazing at the patchwork of towns unfolding beneath us. "This reminds me of when we flew to see the President," she exclaimed, recalling their trip on the Potentia Security business jet. "But this is so much more… open."

I smiled and squeezed Eliana's hand. Soon, though, the excitement of the last few days caught up with her. She nodded off, her head resting on my shoulder. I kept my eyes peeled out the window and listened to the chatter between the co-pilots. It was nothing of interest, just instructions about the helicopter.

As we neared New Delhi, the landscape transformed again. The dense urban clusters of India's capital city spread out below us—a maze of roads, buildings, and green spaces. Soon, the helicopter began its descent, and Eliana woke up, rubbing the sleep from her eyes.

Then, once we landed, another convoy of vehicles waited for us and we found ourselves in a limo. "This is just like the White House limo!" Eliana said, opening up the little fridge and pulling out two water bottles. She handed one to me, which I opened and drank. It was cold, and I realized I had really missed cold beverages.

The convoy of vehicles moved swiftly through the city. The streets of New Delhi were wider and seemed more planned than Mumbai. People still flooded the green tree-lined streets, but it seemed like most were professional, dressed for work, and heading home after a day at the office. The streets were filled with taxis, and I caught sight of buses, and even trains working to move people home.

We pulled into the heart of the city, and massive white buildings with green verdant lawns waited for us.

The driver drove through a gate, rolling down his window and showing a pass, and then we moved toward a stark white building, trimmed with a red brick color. Lush gardens, greener than anything I had seen in West Virginia, spread like a blanket across the property. We had arrived at the official residence of the Prime Minister of India.

We were met by a soldier in full military dress. He smiled and opened the door. "Welcome, please follow me," he said, leading us through a grand archway with security posts on either side. Once we stepped through the official entrance, those same bright green manicured gardens continued. The air was filled with the scent of blooming flowers, some of which were familiar—jasmine, marigolds, and roses. Their colors were vibrant and exotic against the stark white of the building and the green of the vegetation.

We approached the main residence, Eliana and I practically running to keep up with the brisk pace of the soldier. The building was a single-story structure with white walls and a sloping red-tile roof. It had a wide veranda and wouldn't look that out of place in Mt. Storm. It had an air of southern hospitality to it.

The verandas had beautifully carved wooden pillars, and we went straight to the larger building at the end. The passing staff paid us no mind, carrying trays or linens off to somewhere deep in the building.

As we entered, the scent of wood and polish hit us, along with a blast of cold air. Antique wooden furniture and paintings lined the halls, the portraits of past leaders staring at us mysteriously. Ornate tapestries covered some walls, and my fingers itched to reach out and touch them.

We were guided through a large, wood-paneled hallway. The echo of our footsteps blended in with the soft murmur of government officials in the offices that we passed. Eventually, we reached a conference room. A long, polished wooden table dominated the space, surrounded by high-back chairs. I gulped as we approached the far end of the room. The Prime Minister sat, smiling at us, with an enormous flag—orange, white, and green with a spoked wheel in the middle—behind her.

"Sam Silverthorn and Eliana Potentia," the official who had led us here said briskly. "Our honored guests. Please meet Prime Minister Noor Singh."

She rose to meet us. "Welcome," Noor began. "To the great country of India." Her deep-set eyes sparkled with intelligence and kindness. Draped in a richly embroidered garment, with a gold necklace at her throat, she spoke softly. "I've heard so much about you two."

Eliana held out her hand, "Hello, ma'am."

Noor knelt down, placing herself at eye level with Eliana. "Hello, little one. How are you liking India?"

Eliana's eyes sparkled. "It's very nice. I've made a lot of new friends."

With a comforting nod, Noor responded. "I'm so glad my people have shown you hospitality. But I'm sure you would like to return home?"

"Yes, ma'am. I miss my mom and dad, and my best friend, Violet."

"I have been speaking with your mother. She's working tirelessly to ensure your safe return. And I promise, on behalf of India, we'll do everything in our power to get you two back home," Noor said, standing and catching my eye.

My heart swelled with gratitude. I wanted to hug and kiss this woman, but I answered sedately, "Thank you, Prime Minister. Your support means the world to us."

However, Noor's expression turned grave. "I must be transparent with you both." She signaled an aide, who handed over a tablet. She pushed it over to me and I read the text on the screen carefully. It was a communication from US intelligence, demanding the Indian government locate and hand us over to officials at the American Embassy.

"The US President called me," Noor continued. "Demanding that we use Indian resources to track you down. They're desperate, and their methods have become increasingly aggressive."

Eliana's grip tightened on my hand. I pursed my lips, hoping this all wasn't some elaborate trap to get us into their clutches.

Noticing this, Noor offered a reassuring smile, "Do not fear. We have shielded your presence. No one knows where you are."

I've got to admit, the worry and stress from the last few days bubbled up. My voice, filled with urgency, asked, "What's our next move?"

Noor, taking a deep breath, said, "The Limbo gate will be

available to you in two days' time. Until then, you will stay under our protection. You will be guests here at the palace. We must move with caution. This isn't just a matter of traversing realms."

Eliana, ever the beacon of hope, chirped, "Two more days, and then we're going home, right?"

Noor, patting her head gently, replied, "Yes, dear. Two more days. Until then, you will remain here. Let me show you to your quarters, and then you can get settled in. Please dine with me and my family tonight at my personal residence."

We were shown to a suite with one large king bed. "I figured you two would like to sleep together," Noor said as Eliana squealed with delight at a teddy bear in the middle of the bed.

Noor left, and I sat down on the edge of the bed, picked up my cell phone, and dialed Beth. She picked it up on the first ring.

"Beth, you aren't going to believe this, but the Prime Minster of India just invited the two of us to dinner."

"She's a wonderful person," Beth said from thousands of miles away. "Now, how is Eliana?"

Eliana bounded over, the teddy bear clasped to her chest, "I'll be home soon, don't worry."

"I can't help it, sweetheart. The most dangerous part is coming up. Promise me you'll stay with Sam."

"I will, Mom! Don't worry about me. Besides, my magic is getting stronger," Eliana said, sitting down next to me and looking at the phone held in my hand.

"That's what I'm getting worried about. The NSA wants you… bad."

Eliana frowned. "I won't go. I won't let them. I'm coming home."

CHAPTER 23
ESCAPE

Later, we were led through a maze of hallways and tunnels, taking several stairways up to what appeared to be a normal house. Together, we sat in a normal family dining room, and soon, the Prime Minister and her family arrived. Her husband looked like a kind man with thick spectacles and a turban on his head. The two children were teenagers, and Eliana looked at them with enormous eyes.

The room was warm and not overly pretentious. Noor had changed into a simple sleeveless dress and removed her makeup. She spoke to her children about their day, and the two teen boys told her about their school and some tests they had coming up.

As I ate, I listened closely... it sounded no different from a family dinner in the US, although the food was a fragrant vegetable dish instead of meatloaf and mashed potatoes.

Eliana listened intently, keeping quiet as Noor and I talked. I told her about my family, and West Virginia, and she seemed fascinated by the concept of my pack.

Finally, she turned to Eliana after her boys were excused.

"Tell me, Eliana, what's life like for you in the US? I've only read about you in the files and spoken to your mother. I'd love to hear it from you."

Eliana, shuffling her feet a bit, began. "I have a best friend named Violet. We go to Mt. Storm Elementary together. We love playing with dolls and reading books. I just… I just wish things were simple again."

Seeing Noor's questioning gaze, she continued. "I realized my real dad… my biological father, gave me these magic powers. I didn't ask for them. I wish I could just be like any other kid and not have all this… this responsibility and danger around me."

Noor listened patiently, her eyes filled with empathy. "Eliana," she began gently. "Sometimes life places burdens on our shoulders that we didn't ask for. We don't get to choose our parents or the circumstances we are born into. But remember, while some things are not in our control, how we react to them and the choices we make are up to us."

Eliana looked up, eyes filled with the weight of her young years. "But it's so hard."

Noor reached out, taking Eliana's hand in hers. "I can only imagine. But you are blessed, dear child. Not everyone gets a second chance at family. Your adopted parents and your friends would go to the ends of the world for you. That kind of love is rare, and it's a powerful shield against any evil."

Eliana blinked back tears, nodding slowly. "I know. I just wish… I wish things were different."

Noor hugged Eliana gently. "In time, things might be. Until then, remember the love that surrounds you. It's the most potent magic of all."

As Noor and Eliana shared their heartfelt conversation, I watched with a mix of emotions. My family issues gnawed at the back of my mind. As soon as I got back, there would be a reckoning.

Our dinner over, a staff member arrived to take us back to our room. There was no way we could find our way back ourselves, and it was probably wise we didn't wander into places we shouldn't be.

As we rose, I took both of Noor's hands in mine. "Prime Minister Singh, I can't express my gratitude for the support and protection you've extended to us. It's been… a journey I won't forget."

Noor nodded, her gaze shifting to Eliana. "Life has a peculiar way of throwing us into situations we never expect."

I sighed, running a hand through my hair. "You have no idea. I sort of got roped into this whirlwind. One minute, I'm leading my pack, trying to keep everyone happy and fed. The next, I'm trying to protect Eliana."

"You are a good friend," Noor said, smiling down at Eliana, who looked tired from our very long day.

I hesitated for a moment, remembering the circumstances that had led us to this point. "I left my pack, my responsibilities, and now I'm worried about what's happening there in my absence."

Noor's expression remained calm, but the understanding in her eyes was clear. "Leadership is often a heavy mantle to bear, Sam. The constant worry… it's overwhelming. But from what I've seen and heard, you've shouldered this duty bravely."

I smiled weakly, "It's just hard. Especially when you're torn between two worlds."

Noor leaned forward, her voice softening. "Every leader faces moments of doubt and moments where the weight feels unbearable. But remember, it's not just about the decisions we make, but also about the reasons behind them. You're doing this for Eliana, for your pack, and for a greater good. And sometimes, that's all we can do—our best, hoping it'll be enough."

I nodded. It was what I needed to hear. It is funny that I had to go to such great lengths to hear it. "Thank you, Prime Minister. I just hope when we get back, I can make things right."

Noor smiled reassuringly. "One step at a time, Sam. For now, let's focus on getting you both safely home."

The next two days were a flurry of activity. Divya from Mumbai Security, along with Kabir and the rest of her team, came to help with the logistics for the upcoming Limbo gate passage.

As the hours ticked by, I could tell Eliana was getting nervous about our journey home. At breakfast, two days after our meeting with the Prime Minister, she asked me, "Will it hurt, going through the Limbo gate?"

I sighed and took a sip of my tea. "I don't think it's much different from the gate in hell we went through, Eliana. It's just taking us to a different place."

We were interrupted by Divya's arrival. "Good morning! We're set for this evening. I've just received word that the gates are aligning perfectly. We'll head to the location by dusk."

I raised an eyebrow. "Location?"

Divya smiled mysteriously. "It's not just anywhere. The gates align at specific ancient sites. The one we're using is at an old temple, away from the prying eyes of the city."

Throughout the day, we prepared. Divya explained the intricacies of passing through the gate—the rituals to be performed and the chants to be recited. The entire process was steeped in mysticism and tradition.

Eliana grew irritated. "I don't understand why we have to do all this. I can just snap my fingers and it will open."

"I know, dearest. But it's better if we follow the traditions. It makes the priests more comfortable, you know."

"I don't know why we care about the comfort of priests," I chimed in, "We are the ones going through."

Kabir nodded. "You're not wrong, but that is just how it is done. We also need to worry about US agents. They have been spotted around the city. We think they know you are tucked away here."

I had little to say to that. Either we made it through the gate, or we didn't. I was going to do my darndest to make sure they didn't nab us.

As the sun dipped below the horizon, painting the sky in shades of orange and purple, we slipped out of a side gate of the palace, jumping into a waiting unmarked sedan. We set out toward the temple with Divya guiding us. As we neared the site, she slowed down and pulled over on the side of the road.

As Divya had instructed me, I powered down the cell phone and shoved it deep into my pocket. If I left it off, it wouldn't fry when I went through the gate. Then I could turn it back on when we reached our final destination.

Without saying much, we set off down the sidewalk. I was clutching Eliana's hand and keeping my head down. In front of us, Divya walked, clutching a wand under her robes. On the other side, Kabir walked, his head swinging from one side to the other.

We encountered no one on the street and reached the wooded outskirts of the temple compound. A rustling in the bushes caught my attention. Squinting into the twilight, I saw figures moving stealthily behind trees. It was their deliberate movements and coordination that heightened my suspicions.

I whispered to Divya, "We're not alone. I think we have company... and they don't look local."

Divya, taking a deep breath, responded, "Prepare yourselves. I'll try to mask our tracks."

But as we stepped off the pathway and ventured deeper into the temple grounds, we realized these weren't just ordinary pursuers. One figure suddenly threw his hands forward, and a bolt of energy hurtled towards us.

Eliana screamed as Divya quickly deflected it with a barrier spell. Another agent sent a shockwave that caused the ground to shake, sending the shadows sprawling.

I quickly took stock of the situation and transformed into my werewolf form. My heightened senses would be of help, and I quickly located and tackled the attacker. A fierce growl escaped my throat as I held him down. He scrambled up with a force I wasn't expecting, and raised his wand in my direction.

These are not ordinary agents! I thought as I rushed him, knocking him backwards again, and a wand fell out of his hand. He scrambled in the dust to get a hold of it, but I kicked it away.

Eliana, looking panicked, licked her lips in concentration. A protective shield enveloped us. It shimmered in the dim light, deflecting the magical attacks hurled by our pursuers.

Divya, chanting quickly, summoned a mist around us, reducing visibility and allowing us a momentary advantage.

Through the haze, we saw the temple atop the hill, its ancient stone silhouette calling us. Using the mist as a cover, we rushed up the steps. Our pursuers, momentarily disoriented, soon closed the distance, their magical attacks intensifying.

As we neared the temple, Kabir, along with some members of the Indian werewolf pack, emerged, having been alerted by Divya. A massive battle ensued, with magical spells clashing against the strength and agility of the werewolves.

The temple grounds resonated with roars, chants, and the clamor of battle. I kept Eliana safely by my side and defended her fiercely, using my werewolf strength to keep the attackers at bay. I snarled, bit, and slashed at any attacker who emerged from the mist.

Divya, pooling her strength, conjured a blinding light that disoriented the pursuers, giving Kabir's pack an opening to push them back and away from us. Screams and the sound of scrambling feet filled the air.

Kabir and his pack mates returned, their muzzles and claws bloody. I didn't ask if they had killed to protect us. I think I already knew the answer.

All of us were panting and exhausted. We hurriedly entered the temple to proceed with the Limbo gate ritual. Several priests were waiting for us, their faces hidden by orange robes.

Divya paused, her voice almost a whisper. "This is sacred ground. Tread carefully. And remember, whatever you see or hear inside, stay focused on the goal—to pass through the gate safely."

Inside, the temple was lit with oil lamps, their flames dancing and creating shadows that seemed alive. At the center stood an ornate stone archway—the Limbo gate. It looked innocuous, but even I could feel the hum of energy emanating from it.

The priests began the rituals while we stood by, the chants sounding foreign to our ears. The atmosphere grew thick with anticipation, the very air seeming to vibrate.

The stone archway shimmered, and then a bright white light flashed through the room, momentarily blinding us.

"The Limbo gate is open," Divya said. "Hurry, we can't keep it open for long."

I looked down at Eliana. Terror filled her face, and she was shaking like a leaf.

Touching her shoulder, I whispered encouragement, "Come on. It's just Limbo. Nothing there can hurt us."

"Goodbye, Eliana. Goodbye, Sam Silverthorn. Don't forget your friends across the sea," Kabir said, sadness in his eyes.

I stepped up and kissed him quickly on the cheek. "Thank you, Kabir. You are like a brother to me. We won't forget."

And then, taking a deep breath, Eliana and I stepped through the gate.

CHAPTER 24
LIMBO

t was eerily quiet as we stepped through to Limbo. Everything was bathed in a white pearly glow. A long line of people stretched in front of us, waiting to get into the pearly gates.

I looked down at my feet and saw only mist. There were no trees, no buildings, only the soft glow of the gate behind us.

A few hundred feet in front of us, another gate glowed. This must be our exit—the allusive gates we were waiting to line up.

"We have to hurry, Sam," Eliana said, pulling me forward. "One minute in hell is one week outside."

"I know," I said, starting forward, keeping my eye on the long line of people queued up. Something was off about them, and I realized that the endless procession of souls, shimmering and shifting, extended beyond what seemed possible. Each soul waited, some patiently, some with a restless energy, for what appeared to be their chance at Heaven's gates.

At the front, managing the entrance, was a tall, imposing figure with wings that glinted in Limbo's pale light. Saint Peter was unmistakably celestial, but his furrowed brow and the way he massaged the bridge of his nose made it clear he was feeling the stress of management.

"Come on, come on," he grumbled, shuffling souls forward with an impatience that seemed uncharacteristic of a Saint. "We haven't got an eternity. Well, actually, we do, but that's not the point!"

I held Eliana closer, preparing to skirt around the queue. People complained around us. Pointed glares were thrown our way, and I felt suddenly ill at ease.

"Does he even *know* who I am!" one shrill woman, wearing a faded Greenpeace shirt, complained.

"No one cares who you are. Look, before I died, I was a rockstar. No one has even asked me for an autograph," a man with long curly hair said. He had a guitar slung over his back, and he sighed and grabbed it, plucking a few notes while he waited.

But we didn't have time for this. We picked up our pace, practically breaking into a jog.

But we were stopped in our tracks as a woman with long raven-black hair and black thick eyeglasses stepped out of line, blocking our way forward. She had drawn-on eyebrows and wore a flowing housedress. She looked vaguely familiar, but I couldn't place her.

She locked eyes with me, and in that instant, a flood of memories and understanding passed between us. I knew this woman, although not well. She was the reason my father had died, in the same fire that killed her. She was the real mother of the little girl standing beside me. Her name was Lilith Blough, and she was a former psychic for Potentia Security.

I protectively placed a hand on Eliana's shoulder and she looked up at me, confused. Lilith approached us, her gaze shifting to Eliana, who stared back with wide-eyed innocence.

"Who are you?" Eliana said, her voice quivering from fright. She had been only minutes old when her mother died. Of course, she would have no memory. Beth rescued her from the fire and adopted her soon after. Lilith smiled gently, kneeling down to Eliana's height. "Hello, dear one. You have your father's eyes."

Eliana clutched me around the waist, staring at her mother with wide eyes. "You... are my mother?"

Lilith shyly nodded, looking unsure. "You're so big. But I knew you the minute you stepped through the gate. It's almost like someone wanted us to meet," she said, throwing a glance behind her at St. Peter, who had stopped the line and was watching them intently.

"You're dead?" Eliana asked, reaching out a trembling finger. She touched the hem of Lilith's dress, and then drew it back as if it was hot.

Lilith's eyes shimmered with unshed tears. "I am. But time and memory are strange things here." Reaching up, she unclasped a delicate necklace from around her neck—a pendant with a mesmerizing gemstone—and fastened it around Eliana's. "Daughter, I'm sorry. I was led astray. If things had been different... well. No time to second-guess my life. Keep this close to your heart. It will protect and guide you."

From farther down the line, St. Peter left his post. A gasp passed through the crowd as he walked. With each step, he seemed to shrink and transform until he stood next to them at normal height. He was an old man, slightly grumpy-looking, wearing a shiny white robe. Shaking his finger at them, he cleared his throat. "Ahem! As touching as this is, we need to keep things moving,"

Lilith rose, giving Eliana a gentle touch on the cheek. To me, she whispered, "Keep her safe. There's so much she has yet to understand."

St. Peter looked at Lilith kindly, and then said, "Come with me. You are done waiting." Lilith beamed and stepped out of line, following him toward the gate.

She turned around, and with a final, lingering look, she waved goodbye. Then, St. Peter took his spot back at the gates, opened the door, and steered her inside. She beamed, a white shining glow surrounding her, and she slowly faded as she walked through to the other side.

I didn't understand what had really happened. But I clutched Eliana's hand and pulled her toward the gate. "Come on, we've got to go," I said.

Eliana looked down at the pendant on her chest and touched it with her finger. Then she lifted her chin and we both started toward the waiting gate.

Suddenly, Eliana gasped, pointing at the archway. The stone surface rippled like water, and beyond it, we could glimpse another place—green forests, mountains… West Virginia.

I clutched Eliana's hand, and with one last shared look, we stepped through the gate.

Everything spun. Colors and sounds blended in a dizzying whirlwind. And then, as suddenly as it began, it stopped. We were standing in a dense forest, the familiar sounds of home filling our ears.

We had made it.

Eliana laughed, twirling around in glee. "We're home, Sam!"

I let out a relieved laugh, looking around. "Yes, we are. Now, let's find our way back and set things right."

CHAPTER 25
HOMECOMING

Eliana and I emerged from the cool shadows of the Mt. Storm State Park cave. The familiar scent of West Virginia's forests filled our nostrils. The evergreen trees swayed softly as if welcoming us back. With a snap of Eliana's fingers, the magical portal we had just come through closed with a faint shimmer.

I immediately pulled out my phone and powered it on, glad that I remembered to turn it off before going into Limbo. I dialed Beth's number. Within seconds, her voice crackled through, filled with hope. "Sam? Eliana? Is that you?"

"It's us, Beth. We're back," I said, feeling a weight lift from my shoulders.

Moments felt like hours as we waited at the trailhead. The approaching sound of multiple engines broke the silence, and headlights soon appeared. A convoy of SUVs pulled up, and out jumped Beth, Easton, Garret, Dallas, Beau, and Dan. The air was thick with emotions. Relief being the most prominent.

Eliana barely had time to register the events as she was enveloped in a sea of hugs. She caught Beth's eyes shimmering with tears. The strength of their mother-daughter bond was clear.

With her small voice quivering with emotion, Eliana whispered, "Mom, I saw her... my real mom, Lilith."

Beth's eyes widened in shock, and her knees seemed to buckle under her. Tears rolled down her cheeks as she held Eliana even tighter, processing the weight of her daughter's words.

Before the reunion could continue further, Beth's face turned somber. She took a deep breath. "There's something you need to know. The US government... they're trying to take you away, Eliana. They've deemed you a 'potential threat' because of your powers."

Eliana's eyes darkened. The little girl's face contorted in a mix of anger and fear. "I won't go. I'm not their lab rat."

Beth's grip on Eliana tightened, her resolve clear. "We won't let them. You're coming home with me."

Beth turned to me, gratitude in her eyes. "I can't thank you enough, Sam. We owe you more than words can express."

I nodded, feeling distant. Her problems might be over, but mine still loomed. "There might be more trouble on the horizon. Buster, the leprechaun... he might have a role to play in this."

Beth sighed, running a hand through her hair. "I'll handle Buster. He may be a trickster, but he doesn't want to cross me. We'll contact him, but cautiously. No one wants a leprechaun's curse."

With that, the convoy made its way up the winding roads leading to the grand house atop Mt. Storm—home, where a battle of a different kind awaited us.

Standing on the sidewalk, I looked through the big store window. Inside, I knew the hum of hairdryers and the chatter of clients filled the Clip and Cut salon.

I got a little choked up seeing it open like this. When I left, it had still been dark and closed. We had plans for this place, but those were obviously put on hold.

I glimpsed Maggie behind the main counter, ringing up a customer. Not being able to wait a moment longer, I grabbed the door handle, and the bells jingled, signaling my arrival.

Without looking up, Maggie called out, "Just a moment!" But when she did look, she saw me standing there, looking somewhat weary and battle-worn.

Maggie's hands froze mid-air, and the comb she was holding shook. The elderly customer, Mrs. Pritchard, followed her gaze and chuckled. "Looks like you've got someone special there, dear."

Without a word, Maggie gently placed her tools down and rushed over to me, wrapping me in an embrace. Her head rested on my chest, and I bent down and kissed her forehead. The salon fell silent, clients and staff alike witnessing our tender reunion.

When we finally broke apart, Maggie whispered, trying to keep her emotions in check, "I was so scared, Sam."

I brushed a stray lock of hair behind her ear. It had grown out while I was gone. "I'm sorry. It was harder than I thought, but I'm back now."

Maggie bit her lip, trying to hold back tears. "You've no idea how many nights I lay awake, just hoping for any news. The pack has been restless without you."

My face darkened and guilt crept into my voice. "I heard. I'll sort things out."

With a gentle squeeze of Maggie's hand, I continued, "I've missed you, Mags. More than words can say."

The elderly Mrs. Pritchard cleared her throat. "As much as I'm enjoying this romantic drama, my hair…"

Maggie chuckled, wiping away a tear. "Of course, Mrs. P. Let me finish you up."

With a quick word to her assistant, Maggie went back to her station. However, every now and then, her eyes would flit to me as if confirming that I was really there.

After seeing the last of the customers out and flipping the 'Open' sign to 'Closed', Maggie and I went upstairs to our shared apartment above the salon. Glad to be home, I sprawled on my bed, my eyes closed as I hugged my pillow.

The evening was ours—a time to catch up, to be in each other's company, and to find comfort in the fact that, no matter what the world threw at us, we had each other.

CHAPTER 26
BROKEN

awoke with a sense of determination. The first rays of the morning sun streamed through the window, casting patterns on the bedroom floor. Before I could second-guess myself, I reached for my phone on the bedside table, quickly dialing Buster's number at Mt. Storm Motors.

"Morning, Buster," I said as he picked up after a couple of rings. "We need to talk."

There was a brief pause on the other end before Buster replied, "Thought you might call. Come by this afternoon?"

"See you then," I responded, hanging up.

After a quick shower and breakfast, I headed out to the auto body shop where my younger brothers, Frankie and Dennis, worked. As I entered, the familiar smells of oil and fresh paint greeted me. Tools lined the shelves, and a car stood waiting, its hood wide open. My brothers were both bent over the engine, examining it.

"Sam!" Frankie called out in surprise, putting down the tool he was holding and coming over to greet me, a broad grin on his face. Dennis looked up from under the hood and wiped his grease-stained hands, joining in the reunion.

"We were wondering when you'd show up," Dennis said, wrapping me in a tight hug.

Pulling back, my eyes searched theirs, noting the underlying tension. "What's happened since I've been gone?"

Frankie hesitated before responding, "Randy… he's gone, Sam. Found him at the State Park. It wasn't natural. And with you gone…"

Dennis interjected, "Junior saw his chance and has been trying to take over. Mom's been stalling him, but he's been hell-bent on a vote. He's trying to turn the rest of the pack against you."

I shook my head, the gravity of the situation sinking in. "We need to set this right. The Silverthorn pack has to stand for something."

Frankie nodded, "We've been trying, but without you, it's been difficult."

"I'm here now," I stated with a fierce determination. "We'll fix this. Together."

<hr>

The purr of the pickup truck's engine was oddly calming as I navigated my way to Mt. Storm Motors. I had driven this route through town a thousand times, but today, everything looked gray and threatening. I felt out of place and knew that if I didn't fix things soon, it might be too late to fix them at all.

As I parked, I felt the weight of multiple eyes on me. Every salesman seemed to be staring at me with hostility. There was no greeting, no friendly wave, just an uncomfortable silence as they watched me square my shoulders and walk to the front door.

Buster's office was at the back. His door was slightly ajar, and I could see his small frame silhouetted against the window. He didn't look up as I entered, and the air felt heavy and charged.

"Sam," he began without pleasantries. "We had a deal."

Clearing my throat, I gathered my courage. "I know, Buster. But something happened... something I couldn't control. I was pulled into hell."

He chuckled, but it lacked warmth. "Quit the excuses, Sam. Are you trying to dodge out with my coin? You paid that lawyer, and then nothing else. I thought you went on the run."

I pressed on, "I went into hell. It's the truth. You can ask Beth. Eliana and I had quite the adventure. But don't worry, I'll pay back every penny. I just need time."

Buster stood, his eyes narrowing. "Time isn't something I can give freely. You should know that."

For a moment, his jovial, rotund appearance began to warp and twist. Buster's skin became rough and gnarled like the bark of an old tree. His once-bright eyes darkened, now resembling deep, endless pits. His stature grew, and in place of the once-jolly man was a monstrous troll-like creature, towered over me.

My heart raced, every instinct screaming at me to run, but I held my ground, swallowing hard.

The creature's mouth twisted into a sneer. "You see, Sam, there's a beast inside me, and he's not as forgiving as the one you know."

But as suddenly as he transformed, he was back to his usual self. The weight of the room seemed to lift, but I remained rooted to the spot, eyes wide with fear.

"That's what you're dealing with," he whispered. "Now, do we have an understanding?"

I nodded slowly, finding my voice again. "Yes. I'll get you your money."

Buster smirked, leaning back in his chair. "Next time, the beast might not be so forgiving."

"I consider you a friend, Buster. You know I'm good for it. But I need help with the pack." I hated the way my voice sounded, desperate and pleading.

Buster's face went from stern to contemplative. "You ask a lot from me, Sam. First, it's time. Now, it's your pack. Why should I help you?"

"I have nothing to offer but my word," I admitted, eyes sincere. "But you know the Silverthorns. We've been loyal to you, even if things went sideways recently."

After what felt like an eternity, Buster nodded slowly. "Alright. Let's sort this mess out."

Together, we drove to the Silverthorn lands. The winding road that led to the family property was surrounded by the browns of winter. Through the trees, everything was dead and cold. There were no howls to greet me, and for the first time, I didn't feel like I was coming home.

Upon arriving, I wasted no time in organizing a bonfire, howling into the sky, calling my pack. It was time for me to retake my rightful place.

As the flames roared to life, casting dancing shadows on the surrounding trees, the pack members emerged from their homes, drawn to the gathering. The entire Silverthorn pack slowly encircled the fire, their eyes a mix of hope, confusion, and in some cases, hostility. Maggie slipped into the circle, and just seeing her face gave me confidence to do what needed to be done.

I stood tall before them. "I owe you all an explanation," I began, my voice steady but filled with emotion. I recounted my unexpected journey to hell, my adventures with Eliana, and our escape back home.

However, as I spoke, I noticed Junior glowering from the shadows, his presence heavy and threatening. I would not be cowered. Standing tall, I put my hands on my hips, daring him to challenge me.

Junior, his face twisted with anger and resentment, shouted, "You abandoned us, Sam! You have no place here!"

Buster was beside me, and I could sense his growing rage. First, he glowed, and then his face contorted while his body transformed. He roared as the troll within him emerged, his lips twisted into a snarl.

"Enough!" he shouted, his voice echoing throughout the forest, causing some of the wolves to whimper in fear. "You will pay for your treason."

But before anything more could happen, my mother jumped up, putting herself between the monstrous Buster and Junior. To my eyes, she looked frail, and her tear-streaked face was filled with grief.

"No! Buster, please! I've already lost one son! Sam! Tell him!" she cried, clutching Junior protectively.

Buster's fiery gaze locked onto mine, searching for my decision.

I took a deep breath, my voice clear but heavy with pain. "Let him live. There's been enough bloodshed."

The tension in the air was palpable. Buster, with a final warning glare at Junior, reverted to his human form.

Junior took one look around the gathered pack, his face filled with disappointment and bitterness. My pack mates lowered their eyes, refusing to meet his.

"You agree with this? You still want her as a leader after she abandoned us? I thought you were behind me." Junior's bitter words hung in the air as he thumped his chest.

"Sam is the only one who can lead us forward. The mess you have created… well, we don't want any more of the drugs," Randy's widow, Lulu said, tears streaking down her face.

"No. We must find a way forward, however painful," my mother said. She stepped forward and kissed Junior on the forehead. "My blessing on you, but you must leave now. It is for the good of us all."

He glared at me, hatred flowing like a river. I stood defiantly, never breaking my gaze. "Go!" I commanded, pointing to the forest.

Without another word, Junior shifted. He raised his muzzle and howled—a howl filled with pain and sorrow.

And then he was gone, a flash of silver as he disappeared into the woods. He was headed due north. I knew from my own experience that he would find others in the wilderness who had been exiled. And if he was smart, he would make his way to a city and try to blend in. To survive in a human world without a pack was the loneliest thing, but if I could do it, he certainly could.

Without giving my brother another thought, I turned to the fire and considered the flames. "We have work to do." The flames seemed to crackle in response as my pack gathered around me to hear my plans for the future. I took Maggie's hand and spoke again as the leader once more.

Morning would come after the moonshine. It always did.

———

The plot thickens as Sam takes firm control of her pack. But Junior isn't going away, and Buster still wants his money back.

Find out how Sam and friends get out of a hole dug deeper than a leprechaun's horde in Midlife Mountain Mothman. Continue the story here.

Go all the way back to the 80's in a free prequel to the series. Midlife Mountain Magic: The Gates of Hell is a desperate mission to rescue the innocent from the demons below. Claim the story here.

Get The Ebook

ABOUT THE AUTHOR

From rural Indiana, where she had more raccoons and feral cats than neighbors, Renee writes Paranormal Women's Fantasy, which focuses on a main character who is above 40 and has suddenly and inexplicably come into magical powers. Renee, is in fact, 40 plus, and wishes she had magical powers so that she could zap all these annoying menopausal symptoms away. Unfortunately, she will have to settle for a glass of wine and a lapdog.

Milton Keynes UK
Ingram Content Group UK Ltd.
UKHW032326221024
449917UK00004B/365

9 798227 707970